How to Lose an Alien in 10 Days

Alienn, Arkansas 2

FIONA ROARKE

HOW TO LOSE AN ALIEN IN 10 DAYS
ALIENN, ARKANSAS 2

ISBN: 978-1-944312-15-2

For my husband and children
because I love you all so much.

Available Now from Fiona Roarke

BAD BOYS IN BIG TROUBLE

Biker

Bouncer

Bodyguard

Bomb Tech

Bounty Hunter

Bandit

Trouble in Paradise

Barefoot Bay Kindle Worlds

NOCTURNE FALLS UNIVERSE COLLECTION

Aliens Actually

Close Encounters of the Alien Kind

Invasion of the Alien Snatchers

The Alien Who Fell to Earth

ALIENN, ARKANSAS SERIES

You've Got Aliens

How to Lose an Alien in 10 Days

Coming Soon:

My Big Fat Alien Wedding

10 Things Aliens Hate About You

Alexandria Latham Borne is supposed to marry into one of Alpha-Prime's most prestigious families. Her unwanted future fiancé has wealth, breeding, social status...and that's about it. She is less than wowed during their luxury get-to-know-you journey to Earth. Once the spaceship docks in Alienn, Arkansas, Ria jumps at the chance to jump ship and explore the colony of extraterrestrials hiding in plain sight.

Cam Grey takes his job as chief of security at the galactic way station and the Big Bang Truck Stop operated by his family very seriously, but even he needs a break. No one suspects the by-the-book enforcer's secret refuge is the karaoke bar just over the county line from Alienn, Arkansas. It starts out as just another night of uncomplicated amusement. But no one is more surprised than the jaded Alpha when the gorgeous woman with blue-streaked hair sings her way into his bed—and his heart.

When he learns his sexy karaoke singer has defied colony rules, putting them all at risk of discovery by the unsuspecting earthlings, he knows his duty. What he should do is lock her in the brig. What he does do is ignore all the rules he's spent his career upholding.

Cam's also been burned by love before, but his mischievous Ria is a rule-breaker he can't resist.

Is she a heartbreaker, too?

Prologue

Smokin' Hog Saloon, Cooter County in Old Coot, Arkansas

"Come one, come all," the announcer said, his lips caressing the microphone. "Karaoke night starts right now. We'll begin our entertainment with three young lads with a heartfelt message for all the ladies here tonight. Take it away, boys."

Cam Grey entered the Smokin' Hog Saloon, a few miles down the road from the Big Bang Truck Stop on Route 88, just in time to hear that tonight's karaoke performances were about to begin. Perfect. He headed for the back of the rustic place, skirting the eating tables with simple wooden tops and chairs to match, and passed through the large doorway into the lounge. There were two pool tables on the left. He might avail himself of a game or two, if the karaoke performances were sucky.

He found his favorite karaoke viewing seat empty and walked to a low sofa beneath a large picture window on one wall. Through the window,

Cam could see Maxwell the Martian hanging off the flying saucer-shaped Alienn, Arkansas water tower in the distance. Perfect line of sight to Alienn and also for his communication needs.

He wasn't too far from home, but he might as well be a hundred miles away—this was earthling territory and out of greater Alienn, just over the city limits line and into Cooter County.

Cellular signals worked well here, but more importantly, Cam's communicator was still in range of Alienn's closed system. The earthling karaoke bar and grill was as far as he could go without being out of reach of the lower level of the Big Bang Truck Stop. That would be hard to explain.

Diesel—well, all of his brothers, really—had to practically make a federal case out of leaving the area to go "out of town" for any reason. Out of town really meant out of communication range of their underground galactic way station.

The Smokin' Hog Saloon offered a slice of earthling entertainment without the need to announce to the township of Alienn where he was going or what he was doing. His brothers would likely be shocked to find out he spent time here, but he loved it. The karaoke, and the privacy.

Thursday night was ladies' night, though men were allowed to sing, too. He enjoyed seeing drunken earthlings get up the nerve to sing popular tunes in front of the typically raucous crowd.

A difficult memory traipsed across his mind, a recollection of the fool he'd been over a human woman he'd met in this very bar. While that story had ended poorly, and had given him a new attitude and a tough shell where love was concerned, Cam kept coming back because he wanted to prove to himself—and others—that the search for true love and happily ever after was a useless endeavor.

He didn't need it. He didn't want it. He could live his life perfectly well all alone.

Cam had gotten right back up on the horse of life and found he liked the singular view. Since that one romantic disaster, his relationships were short, enjoyable and never repeated with the same girl. After two years of riding this particular steed, his outlook hadn't changed much. Well, maybe a little.

Diesel had fallen in love with an "out of town" earthling. Cam had tried to warn his brother it wasn't a good idea. He told him to hurry and get the human out of his system. Diesel hadn't listened, of course, but that affair had turned out surprisingly well despite Cam's warnings that love with an earthling was a bad idea.

As it turned out, Diesel's new love interest wasn't all human, so Cam felt justified in his continued judgment that Alphas and earthlings shouldn't fall in love or co-mingle with the idea of permanence or any such foolishness.

Short-term affairs with no strings attached from the get-go were a completely different matter.

The Smokin' Hog was a bit quiet for ladies' night, but it was early. Perhaps more folks would show up as the night progressed. Cam searched the vicinity for the waitress to order a drink, motioning her over when she looked in his direction. The waitress quickly brought his beverage of choice. He sipped his beer and settled in to watch the show.

The small stage held a microphone attached to a stand, complete with an old-fashioned cord snaking off toward the karaoke machine. Totally old school.

The first act of the evening was three drunken college boys singing *You've Lost That Loving Feeling,* not the first time he'd seen that particular performance, or likely the last. None of the trio looked like Tom Cruise or a Top Gun candidate, but they were entertaining.

Next up was a shrunken dude—who had to be a hundred and eight if he was a day—singing *I'm Too Sexy*. He was most assuredly not. The highlight of his set had to be when he ripped his shirt open at the end of his dubious performance. An old tattoo across his chest in droopy, once-black block letters clearly revealed his tribute to MOM. Awesome.

Finally, the ladies began to take the stage. One woman belted out a not terrible solo of *I Will Survive,* and a flashy, raucous trio laughed and sang their way through a version of *Walk Like an*

Egyptian. They managed to lure everyone in the karaoke bar area—except Cam—into trying to mimic the girls on stage and walk like an Egyptian. Some managed much better than others. Mostly, it was comical to watch.

He noticed a pool table was open. Sometimes by now he was ready for a game because the music was either unmemorable or really terrible. Tonight, he ignored the open pool table, settled in and waited.

The bartender called out the name of the next singer. Ria.

It was an interesting name. Ria. He liked it.

Cam took a sip of his beer as the participant crossed the room to the stage. He heard wolf whistles and catcalls before looking up to see an utterly enchanting female.

Ria was tall, dark-haired and slender, but had lovely curves in all the right places. Notably, several strands of her hair were streaked with rebellious bold blue. He *really* liked that.

She grinned at him as she passed his table on her way to the stage. He lifted his beer glass in salute. She lifted her purple martini glass in his direction. Once on stage, she put her drink on a table next to the karaoke machine, grabbed the microphone off the stand and put in her selection.

The first notes of music poured from the karaoke machine and Cam was transfixed. She stared at him and only him. It was as if they were the only two people in the room.

She sang a beautiful and soulful rendition of *Need You Tonight.* He was immediately smitten. Every note, every crescendo only served to enamor him further. *"...cause I'm not sleeping,"* she sang. He didn't think he'd be *sleeping tonight* either. He hadn't felt like this in...well, a couple of years. Even the memory of his disastrous previous relationship with another earthling didn't sway him from wanting this stunning female.

The woman named Ria, singing directly to him and no one else, touched Cam on a level no one else had ever reached. He couldn't take his gaze off her. He considered inviting her to join him for a drink. As she continued singing, he revised his plan. He wanted to invite her to his home. He had the next few days off. Perhaps he'd bend his personal rule and invite her to stay longer than a single night.

If she was willing, they could spend the entire weekend together...*not sleeping*.

Chapter 1

Early the next morning

Cam came awake the moment his communicator buzzed on the nightstand. The first thing he felt was a warm body snuggled against his side. The first thing he saw when he opened his eyes was a thick strand of blue-streaked hair curled invitingly over his bare chest. He inhaled deeply and a newly familiar perfume filled his lungs.

Ria, the luscious karaoke singer. Memories of the night before filtered into his brain one by one, bringing with them a relaxed, satisfied attitude. After she finished her song, the crowd gave her a standing ovation and quickly requested she sing another.

Her cheeks colored prettily. She seemed surprised by the audience's vocal approval, but she complied with a soulful, angst-filled rendition of Heart's *Alone*. Again, she sang for Cam. Again, it felt like they were the only two in the room. He liked it.

As the last notes faded and the audience clapped and hollered their approval, she came straight to Cam's table and sat next to him on the sofa. She mashed her leg up against his from knee to hip as if they were already involved and couldn't keep from sucking together like magnets when they got close. He liked that, too. A lot.

Her gaze never strayed far from his face the entire time they spoke. He couldn't quite remember the details of what they'd discussed, but she eagerly accepted his invitation to spend the coming weekend with him. Her lovely hazel eyes lit up the moment he suggested a more intimate setting for a further discussion.

Cam's communicator sounded stridently once more, rattling across the surface of his nightstand and bringing him back to the present. He recognized the caller on the number display, picked it up and answered, "What?" He tried not to sound as grumpy as he felt over the interruption.

"Cam!" Axel, his typically happy-go-lucky brother, sounded uncharacteristically uptight and worried. "Thank heavens you answered! You've got to come here right now!"

"Come where?" He glanced at the clock on his nightstand, grimaced when he realized he'd only been asleep for about two hours. It was not enough rest, according to the ache growing inside his head, no matter how pleasant the reason for his lack of sleep.

"To the passenger lounge," Axel said impatiently, as though he expected Cam to read his mind. That wasn't going to happen, especially not on so little sleep.

"Why?" Cam began to mentally drift as he waited for an answer.

"There is someone missing. Someone important."

Cam's eyes opened and his brain did, too. "Missing from Alienn?"

"No! Why would I care about that? A *passenger* is missing from the *Royal Caldera Forte* cruise liner! They are set to depart in less than two hours, but they obviously can't leave until the missing passenger is found."

Cam glanced at Ria, head resting on his shoulder. She seemed sound asleep. He didn't typically discuss below stairs issues when he was entertaining, but found he didn't want to move to a more private location. Her warmth felt too good curled against his side.

"I thought they were leaving after the weekend. Was there a schedule change?"

"Yes. There was a significant volcano blast on an uninhabited planet along the route. Didn't you get that memo?" Axel didn't give Cam time to answer. "They'll lose a day each way going around it. The eight days out just became ten days because they are losing the weekend here. And now with this missing passenger, this has become a veritable space potato storm about to hit an industrial-sized fan. Are you on your way yet?"

Ria stirred. Sliding her palm tantalizingly across his chest, she hooked a hand around his other shoulder and hugged him even closer. He looked into her sleeping face. She sighed, smiled and sent his attention blasting into several incredible memories from the night before. He gently grabbed a fistful of her rich, soft hair and kissed her forehead. He wished he could go back to sleep snuggled up against Ria. Or maybe wake her up…

Axel shouted, "Cam! Are you still there?"

He sighed. "Yes. Still here." *But I'd rather be re-living my memories and creating new ones.*

"Are you on your way?" Axel asked again. "Please come and help me. I'm in the passenger lounge with… *Director Patmore.*"

Cam stifled a groan. Since Axel whispered the name, Cam guessed the man in charge of passengers on the *Royal Caldera Forte* must be within earshot. He really had no choice.

"Okay. Fine. I'll be right there." He disconnected and eased away from Ria. If it were anyone but Axel, he might have brushed them off and told them to figure it out. However, Axel didn't often get so riled. He was the most easygoing of Cam's five brothers.

Plus, Patmore was a real "pain in the patootie," as his unconventional aunt Dixie often said about difficult people. Smiling to himself, he amended the mental phrase to, "*Patmore* is a pain in the patootie." He attributed his goofy attitude to the woman snuggled up in his bed. For the first time in a long time, he had a happy start to his day. He dressed quickly, intending to rescue Axel, but not stay in the basement of the Big Bang Truck Stop any longer than he had to.

He leaned down and kissed Ria's cheek. She opened one eye and saw him fully clothed. Dismay filled her features. The other eye opened drowsily. "Are you leaving me already?" she asked in a husky, totally sexy, voice.

"Only for a little while. I have to take care of something at work, but I'll be back as fast as I can. Okay?"

She pushed out a sigh, snuggled her face into his pillow and said, "Okay. I'll just wait here, then."

Ria was asleep by the time he whispered, "Good, because I'm not nearly finished with you yet." He kissed her temple, breathing in her delectable scent once more. Biting back a groan of delight and the urge to climb back in bed, Cam exited his room, pausing in the doorway for one last look at the sexy woman. He hated to leave. Every fiber of his being wanted to ignore Axel and crawl back into bed, snuggle up and get more sleep.

He frowned. When had *that* ever happened before? Well, there was that one other time. He dismissed the bad memory and all the baggage that accompanied it. He truly was over his last disastrous relationship. He *knew* he was over it, because he desperately wanted to wake Ria up, kiss her senseless and repeat every moment of last night. It was a sensation resurrected from the time *before* he'd been hurt, and he liked that quite a lot. Maybe Ria and her blue-streaked hair and lust for life had cured him of his forlorn outlook on love with earthlings. He took a step toward the bed.

Cam remembered the extreme tone of Axel's worry. He needed to go. If he didn't leave now, he wouldn't. Pushing out a resigned sigh, he turned on his heel and exited his home. He'd take care of this problem quickly and return to Ria. It was likely a passenger miscount. It had happened before.

Axel didn't typically take care of the passenger manifests. As head of security, that was Cam's job. He cut his brother some slack and quickened his pace. His house wasn't far from the Big Bang Truck Stop and the underground facility that housed all of their secret alien technology and served as a way station for passing cruise ships and other spacecraft from Alpha-Prime.

Cam parked his SUV haphazardly in the employee lot and strode through the secret underground entrance, quickly making his way to the passenger lounge. His brother stood with the annoying director and a woman from the cruise liner's elite First Class deck. He'd seen her the day before when the passengers disembarked upon their arrival. She looked at their simple way station like she wasn't certain she wanted any of Earth's air to taint her expensive clothing or her person.

Axel appeared to be more than relieved when he saw Cam. He raced to his side, talking a mile a minute. "Good to see you, Bro. What took you so long?"

Cam opened his mouth, but Axel interrupted. "Never mind. Doesn't matter. You're here now." He didn't take a breath, just continued, "So I've done two tallies and Director Patmore did his own secondary count after his initial discovery of the discrepancy. All four of the totals say we are missing one person.

"The director's count was obviously more detailed, so he actually came up with a name while you were on your way here. Turns out it's a missing girl. The lady next to the director is the mother."

Cam immediately felt sick he hadn't rushed to get here. "Are you telling me a child is missing? Why didn't you mention that before?"

"Because she's not a child, she's an adult. But she's the daughter of a former Governor and her widowed mother is *very* distraught."

Cam relaxed a notch. He was less concerned the person in question was the daughter of the Earth equivalent of a wealthy VIP, and more concerned she was actually missing. "Okay. What's the name of the missing *adult* girl?"

Axel looked at a piece of gray paper in his hand. "Her name is Alexandria Latham Borne, which sounds like the name of a princess to me, but her mother is about to come right off the rails and the director is threatening all sorts of dire things if we don't find her pronto and—"

"Right, I got it. Relax, Axel. Take a breath. She can't be too far away. The cruise liner only docked yesterday afternoon."

His brother inhaled deeply and let out a long exhalation. "Okay. Yes. Only yesterday. You're right. What's next? What should we do?"

Axel must be extremely rattled if he didn't immediately grasp the most obvious next step. "Do they have a picture of her?"

His brother nodded. "The mother said she brought one, but I haven't seen it yet. She was waiting for the 'actual' man in charge of security, not the fill-in guy." He rolled his eyes and Cam got a much clearer picture of the person he was about to deal with. He sighed internally and bore up to hate this coming conversation.

Cam and Axel joined the director and the Governor's wife.

"Are you the one *actually* in charge of security here? Are you here to find my baby?" the woman demanded, managing in one short exchange to sound stricken and dress him down for not working twenty-four seven. "I'm so worried about her. We must find Alexandria. Her future fiancé, Douglass Barnard FitzOsbern—who is a Technician's son, by the way—is beside himself with worry." Given that

Douglass Barnard FitzOsbern wasn't in attendance, Cam wondered if that was the truth. Not that it mattered. An Alpha-Prime Technician was at the top of the social tier, definitely wealthy, and deference was always accorded to such VIPs and their associates.

Director Patmore broke in to make the formal introductions. "This is Governess Ruth Latham Borne, wife of the late former Governor Robert Borne.

"Governess Latham Borne, this is Cam Grey, the primary security officer for this Alpha colony way station facility."

Cam was typically good at reading people. He couldn't read the minds of Alphas like he could humans, but he had a better-than-average feeling for what motivated people. This situation was no different. He took one look at the mother of the missing girl and had her figured out before she spoke another word.

Ruth Latham Borne was obviously upset. And while she said one thing, she was worried about something else entirely. He needed to figure out what, but suspected he understood *exactly* what was going on here.

She was a Governor's widow, part of the upper middle class, while her daughter's fiancé was a part of the elite Archetech class.

A Technician was as good as lower-end royalty, after Planner and Designer, but royalty nonetheless.

Cam had the rest of the story figured out in about two seconds.

The Governor's daughter didn't want to marry the Technician's son—surely a lucrative arranged marriage, from her mother's point of view—and she'd run off in protest or to escape a less-than-appealing fiancé. This wasn't the first time an arranged marriage had been thwarted, but the event was rare.

The old traditions—popular or not—held firm sway with many folks, and he guessed Governess Latham Borne was no different.

Cam didn't blame her, nor did he plan to lose any sleep or any more personal time dealing with what he considered manufactured drama. Alas, protocol dictated he couldn't say what was *really* on his mind. Instead he took a more disciplined attitude. "Everything that can be done will be done to find your daughter, Governess Latham Borne. Do you know *why* she might have run off?"

"What makes you think she ran off?" The woman's acidic tone came very fast on the heels of her *I'm a heart-wrenched, worried mother* attitude of a few moments ago.

The director's eyebrows went straight to his hairline. "Madam, did you have knowledge that your daughter might have disappeared on purpose?"

"Of course I have no such knowledge," she said unconvincingly, sniffing deeply several times as if she'd just developed an allergy to telling lies. "That's preposterous."

"Oh? Really? Does your daughter suffer from an arranged marriage, by any chance?" Cam asked bluntly.

Governess Latham Borne drew herself up to her full height and said imperiously, "Be that as it may, she needs to be found. Immediately. What are you going to do about this situation, Security Man?" Her tone implied she substituted the word "servant" for "security" in her head.

Cam wanted to answer, "Big fat nothing!" but he cleared his throat, ignored her intended slur and said, "Do you have a picture of your daughter?"

She pulled a paper thin, transparent, postcard-sized Alpha-Prime photo generator from the pocket of her expensive caftan, swiped the bottom edge a few times to find the right image and handed it to him. Cam glanced at the upside-down picture and noted a dark-haired figure dressed in equally expensive clothing, but didn't study it. He simply placed his communicator over the surface, pushed a button and drew his device across it, transferring the image.

He handed the device back to Governess Latham Borne and gave his communicator to Axel.

"Make a copy for yourself and then distribute it wide to our search personnel."

"Wait!" Governess Latham Borne put her hand to her chest, adding dramatically, "You can't do that."

"Why not?" Axel asked.

"I will not allow my daughter's photo to be circulated like she is some gulag-bound criminal. No. Absolutely not! That course of action is completely out of the question. I do not give my permission to have her picture *circulated*." Governess Latham Borne said the word like she had to hold her nose to utter the stench-worthy verb.

Cam narrowed his gaze. "What do you expect me to do? Carry her picture around to every home in the state of Arkansas and look for her all by myself?"

Her half-shrug suggested that was exactly what she expected. "That's your job, isn't it, *Security* Man?" Her disdain again came through clearly in her tone. Cam had news for her. He was no one's servant.

The director stepped between them and tried a more reasonable tone. "I'm sorry, madam, but wide circulation is the typical protocol in a missing person case. Several people looking for your daughter all at once will yield results faster than only one operator out and about searching."

"She's not a missing person. She's my daughter who is more simply lost on a peculiar, uncouth planet. There's no telling what might have happened to her with bands of humans rambling around causing trouble. Listen to me closely, as I will not repeat myself. I want her found without some backward colony security lowlife ruining her pristine reputation. Can I assume that I am understood in this matter or do we need to contact Alpha-Prime's Technician League for guidance?"

The Technician League was powerful, but wouldn't give a rip about a missing Governor's daughter on a far-off planet. Even so, Cam decided silence was the best response.

He turned away from the woman's imperious stare and sent Axel a look that said, "Sheesh. Rich people." The corners of Axel's lips turned up slightly.

The director, as disagreeable as he typically was, gave Cam a distinctly uncomfortable look of remorse. He pulled both Axel and Cam to the side, out of earshot of his imperious guest. "Please don't mistake her...well, obvious concern and angst about her daughter for anger. You see, Governess Latham Borne doesn't understand our established search procedures and—"

"Don't worry, Director. I get it," Cam said, forcing calm into his tone. She was rich. She was used to having every wish she expressed carried out instantly and without question and every demand she uttered satisfied immediately, if not sooner. "She's upset about her missing daughter and the circumstances of her disappearance. I won't take offense."

The director nodded, taking the gracious out Cam offered. Cam understood completely, that the woman had no regard for anyone's feelings or workload, but he didn't plan to give in to her foolish demands.

"We'll search a few places first-time visitors to Earth have been known to frequent and linger at, then report back in an hour or so. If she returns to the ship on her own in the next sixty minutes, please notify Axel immediately. He's taking point on this matter." Axel's eyes widened in an expression that said, "Who? Me?"

"Yes. Of course. Thank you," the director said.

Cam was about to say, "Don't thank me. Axel is the only one who will be searching. I'm going home to someone delicious," when he brought up the picture of Alexandria Latham Borne on his communication device. He studied the wealthy girl's general physique, noting she was every inch the rich, expensively groomed Governor's daughter. Wearing what had to be an expensive cranberry-colored designer outfit from Alpha-Prime, the young woman in the photo seemed to say, "I'm privileged and I know it."

His gaze slid to her face, expecting to see a haughty, superior expression. Instead, he saw very familiar rebellious hazel eyes and a mischievous smile.

Cam's heart stuttered then flipped over in his chest. He brought the photo nearer, as if closer examination would change it. It didn't. It was her.

There were no blue streaks in her hair, but it was definitely the sexy woman sleeping in his warm bed, waiting for his return.

"I bet you'll find her first," Axel said.

Normally, Cam would have said, "I'll take that bet."

But not today.

Chapter 2

Ria had no trouble falling back to sleep after Cam left to "take care of something" at work after a call disturbed them. He said he'd be right back in a tone that suggested they might not be sleeping when he returned. She needed a couple more hours to recover from all the lost sleep from the night before, even though the lack had been totally worth it.

She thought she managed to mumble something about waiting here. She must have, because he whispered, "Good, because I'm not nearly finished with you yet." She'd tried to smile, but dropped off. Last night with Cam had been beyond her wildest expectations.

She didn't know how long he'd been gone when the doorbell started ringing. She sincerely wanted to ignore it, but the person outside seemed rather insistent. After what seemed like an endless stream of blaring noise, Ria shrugged on Cam's shirt from the night before and shuffled to the entrance. She briefly fumbled with the unfamiliar locking mechanism, then opened the door halfway. The light of day almost blinded her, forcing her eyes mostly closed before she blinked hard in an effort to block some of the extreme sunlight.

Ria guessed the elderly woman on the stoop to be Cam's neighbor when she started with, "Finally, you answer your door, Cam. I need to know if you have—" The woman stopped speaking, eyed Ria wearing Cam's shirt and apparently nothing else, her gaze traveling from the top of her messy, slept-on head of hair down to bare, painted toes. She grinned and said, "Oh. Well, then. Never mind," and abruptly turned and walked away. Ria stood at the open door all alone with no idea what the older woman needed from Cam. Whatever.

Not that Ria could have supplied anything like a cup of sugar—wasn't that what all earthling neighbors asked for when they came over?—or even a coherent spoken word, as it turned out.

I should have just stayed in bed.

Ria, eyes closed for the short journey, made her way by feel alone back to the bedroom and Cam's comfy bed, and slipped under the covers ready to conk out again. She luxuriated in the soft texture of sheets surrounding her and the remarkable scent Cam had left on his pillow. She buried her face in his pillowcase, breathing deeply before drifting into oblivion.

Some time later, she had no idea how long and didn't care, Cam returned.

She woke when he called out, "Ria!" *Ooh, that yummy voice makes my toes curl.*

Ria was barely awake, but the heated memories of their decadent night swirled in her mind. She never wanted to leave. She could be perfectly happy right in this bed from now on. She wouldn't have to hide the blue streaks she'd put in her hair before sneaking off the *Royal Caldera Forte*. She could dress how she wanted and do what she wanted and live how she wanted. This was fun. This was freedom. This was where Ria wanted to stay forever. Plus, she couldn't move yet even if she wanted to, she was that sleepy and worn out from last night's best fun ever.

He yelled her name a second time, but sounded closer to the bedroom. Ominously, he added, "We need to have a talk."

Oh no. She didn't want to talk. She wanted to *do* something. She wanted to recreate last night's breathtaking experience.

Unfortunately, Cam didn't sound happy. Did he have to work? Was he about to kick her out because he had a marvelous Earth life he needed to get back to? He couldn't have found out who she was and where she'd run from, could he? Surely not. Earthlings were kept in the dark about alien things on this planet. Whatever he wanted to *talk* about, she knew she wasn't ready to leave. If he had to work, she'd stay here until he was finished.

She focused her sleepy mind on being

persuasive. She'd have to convince him to let her stay for the weekend, even though she wasn't supposed to be this far from the way station. Come to think of it, she didn't even know where she was or how far away the way station was. Her mind had been otherwise engaged last night, and she hadn't paid attention.

Ria pretended to be asleep when Cam came in. She heard him move to her side of the bed. The mattress dipped as he plopped down next to her. Perfect.

"Ria. Wake up. We need to talk about something important." He put a firm hand on her shoulder, squeezing gently, the tone of his voice softer now that he was so close. The only important thing she wanted to discuss was the itinerary for the coming few days they'd be together.

She slowly opened her eyes and stared deeply into his blue gaze for several seconds before whispering, "Good morning, Cam." She kept staring, trying to get him to forget whatever he was about to say. His eyes—which seem wise beyond their years—softened.

A half-smile shaped his gorgeous mouth. "Good morning, Ria." He inhaled and then exhaled, looking much less stressed than he'd sounded when he'd arrived. Maybe her persuasion was working.

She studied his dark blond hair for a moment, remembering how soft it was when she'd slipped her fingers through it. "Did you sleep well?" she asked, than added, "I hope so. I slept like the dead, in case you wondered, but I'm still exhausted."

Cam relaxed a bit more, his shoulders easing down a notch. "I slept much the same, until I got interrupted. I'm worn-out, too, but I also have no regrets."

Her tummy made an opportune noise in that next moment. Cam's gaze went to where the noise came from. He put his hand there, rubbing her stomach through the shirt she wore. *His* shirt. He seemed to note this as he stroked her belly. One corner of his luscious mouth lifted in seeming approval. "This shirt looks better on you than it does on me." She thought it looked good on both of them.

Ria wanted to keep him from declaring whatever "important" thing he wanted to discuss. "Didn't you mention something about breakfast last night and how you were going to bring it to me in bed?" Ria asked, even though she would rather do something else entirely in bed.

His body seemed to relax further. Her persuasion was working. He didn't seem as intense or ready to discuss whatever important thing he'd come in to say. "I seem to remember something like that, yes."

His half-smile widened into a full-blown grin. Ria sat up and kissed him gently on the lips. He kissed her back, ardently. "Come back to bed, Cam," she whispered. "Belly growling aside, I'm not really hungry for food. Not yet, anyway. Get undressed and snuggle with me for a little while, okay?"

He paused, as if torn. She saw the moment he capitulated in his eyes, before he said, "Okay. But just for a little while." Her persuasion worked again. Excellent. She planned to sway him for the next three days, until she had to go back to the ship.

He stood and peeled off his T-shirt, revealing his rocking hot upper body. *Whew*. His hands lowered to his waistband and she licked her lips. A jarring buzzing sound stilled his fingers on the button just as he began to unfasten it. He sighed and pulled a communication device out of his pocket.

He looked at the screen and made an odd face.

"Who is it?"

Cam pushed out a long sigh. "My crazy aunt."

"Shouldn't you answer it?"

"I'd rather not."

"Why?"

"Did I mention the part about where she's crazy?"

She giggled and one corner of his beautiful mouth lifted in amusement. "I don't have the fortitude to deal with her foolish antics so early in the morning. She'll have to bother one of my other family members." He stared down at the buzzing device, indecision clearly weighing on his mind. Meanwhile, Ria stared at his abs, his chest and his amazing profile. She wanted to hiss in pleasure merely looking at his gorgeous physique.

Cam sat on the bed, device in hand, but watched her as if the noisy buzz-ringing in his hand had gone away.

She sent a mental push for him to forget his device. She'd heard it worked on most earthlings. Was it working on him? Maybe. His focus remained squarely on her.

Ria sat up, inched closer to him, and began to kiss his bare shoulder as he listened to the strident buzz-ring. She trailed kisses from his shoulder to the back of his neck, licking a spot she had learned he liked. He dropped the device. She heard it bounce on the carpet, but Cam didn't reach for it. He turned to stare deeply into her eyes. She sent another mental push to urge his cooperation. Smiling serenely, she pushed a mental message with her gaze for him to ignore anything and anyone but her.

The buzzing ring of his communications device stopped momentarily, but started up seconds later.

Ria leaned close and placed a gentle kiss on his jaw. Cam ignored his phone completely to kiss her hard on the mouth. He pushed her flat on the bed's surface and followed her down without breaking the carnal kiss.

She scraped her nails gently down the center of his back. He broke the kiss to growl his approval before resuming the seductive kiss. Cam was an earthling, but he was built just like an Alpha. She appreciated his large, muscular build. Earthlings were very similar to Alphas, but her alien race was often superior in average stature. Not Cam. There was absolutely nothing average about him.

A final faint half buzz-ring came from the floor. If Cam heard it, he ignored it. After several seconds, the caller apparently gave up and the buzzy-ringing stopped. By that time, they were rolling around on the bed, kissing like tomorrow didn't exist for them. The truth was, it might not.

Tomorrow with Cam might only be a wish. If anyone discovered her missing from the cruise liner, further exploring of any kind might not happen at all. If she could continue to persuade Cam to forget everything in his life except her, she might be able to enjoy the entire weekend. But she'd eventually have to go back. Ria didn't like it, but it was the truth. Unless someone came for her before then.

It was only a matter of who might show up. One, the human authorities on this wonderful planet; two, the way station security personnel; or, three, her mother leading the way with Director Patmore trailing her and Dirt Bag FitzOsbern bringing up the rear. She shoved those horrendous visions to the back of her mind and swore not to think about that eventuality until it was forced upon her.

Cam began to ease away from the luscious kiss, but Ria tunneled her fingers into his soft, silky hair and instigated an even more volatile lip lock. He responded in kind. She hummed in her throat. This was exactly the way last night's adventures had started, with a kiss.

Well, there'd been a song or two first and then a drink or two, and finally a kiss or two or a dozen. Likely she should be more worried about the eventual discovery of her absence from the ship, but she vowed to only leave this bed kicking and screaming. If anyone dared make her go, that someone was going to have to drag her out. She'd fight tooth and nail.

For now, she pretended she was an Earther who didn't have a care in the world. She pretended no one would ever look for her or come after her. The price for her disobedience would certainly be quite hefty, but the kiss she shared with Cam was well worth all of what she'd done—or would do—in the name of stubborn self-preservation and the desire to select her own mate to share a lifetime *she* chose.

Becoming an Earther, as the Alpha-Prime colonists on Earth were called, and spending the rest of her life with an earthling was her secret goal. Cam was the perfect choice. Being with him now was an excellent start to her defiant plan. If she got to keep him.

Cam was everything she'd ever dreamed of in a lifelong partner and so much more. She'd taken one look at him in the earthling bar and known he would be important. The more she learned, the more she liked. They were great together, impeccably suited in temperament, and they had identical ideas of entertainment. From the moment she sat down, crowding next to him as if they were already acquainted, they had connected, laughing and joking together. He told her she had a voice like an angel, even though it was her very first karaoke experience.

With the all-important attraction gene—the one that created an arc between them whenever they talked, kissed or wildly rolled around on his sheets—clearly present, all of these compatibilities demonstrated they should be together. She didn't want to think about any future other than this idyllic one she'd built in her mind. He was the perfect earthling.

And Cam was enamored of her, too. At least he was for now, thanks to her mental encouragement of his affections.

Ria tried not to remember she might have his attention now, but it wouldn't last. She had a day, two at best, and then her limited power of persuasion over him would fade. Her rebellious actions would certainly become public and she might have to return to life on another planet far, far away, with no choice, no fun and, worst of all, no Cam.

In the meantime, she planned to take advantage of every second with him she could carve out. If she had her way—and she wouldn't—she'd move in with Cam, marry him, and spend the rest of her life here on Earth doing whatever earthling things he liked to do.

The reality of her future loathsome existence would come barging in soon enough. Until then she would relish every second away from the outline others had created for her life, casually expecting her to follow it to her ultimate doom. The longer she spent away from the ship, the stronger her anger became over what others had decided. That anger stiffened her resolve to thwart what others had decreed, even if only for a single wonderful weekend.

If her mother forced her to marry Douglass Barnard FitzOsbern—or rather, Dirt Bag FitzOsbern, as she'd nicknamed him—Ria would make it her life's mission to ensure everyone in the situation was as miserable as she expected to be.

Chapter 3

Cam woke for a second time to the sound of his communication device buzzing from somewhere nearby. His eyes opened, but he didn't spy it on his nightstand. Listening, he realized it was still on the floor on Ria's side of the bed. He carefully crawled over her and answered it, putting the device to his ear as he settled on his belly, crunched up next to Ria's warm side.

"Yep." Ria had stirred as he slid across her soft body. She reached out a hand, which landed on his back. He loved her touch. The softness of her fingertips absently stroking the muscles along his spine made him want to drop the phone and return to cuddle with her. Even as he knew what that would lead to soon enough.

"Cam!" It was Axel again.

"What?"

"Where are you?"

He almost said, "In bed," but managed to say, "Home. Why?"

"Home? Still? Did you even look around at all?"

His brother's accusatory tone distracted him from Ria and her magical touch.

"Look around? For what?" He cleared his throat and paused a few seconds, trying to catch up. It didn't work. His mind lingered on Ria. She scratched her nails down his back lightly, and he felt the thrill of it to his bones. "What's up?" he finally asked.

Cam was barely awake. His strength had been sapped by the beautiful, enthusiastic karaoke singer he'd brought home. She was amazing. He was spent and exhausted like he'd never been before. Honestly, the long weekend he planned to spend with her might not be enough. He didn't want to even think of a future without her in it.

Dangerous territory for him, given his past, but it was what it was.

"You know exactly what's up." The sound of Axel's incredulity seemed oddly out of character.

He cleared his throat and said, "I forgot. Tell me again."

Cam heard a long sigh from the other end of the line. In a perturbed tone, Axel said, "No need to tell you again. I called to tell you to never mind. Also, thanks for nothing."

"What is your problem?" Cam mumbled, not really caring if he got an answer, trying to stay conscious to finish the conversation.

"We found the missing person, no thanks to you. So you can go back to your day off."

"Great. Glad it worked out." Cam managed the few placating words that rolled off his tongue without effort, not really meaning them or even knowing what he said. He was tired. Drained of energy for the best possible reason. Besides, it *was* his day off. He worked hard. He deserved time away from work every now and again. He was never going to apologize for living his life the way he wanted to. But he also didn't share much about how he lived his life with anyone.

"Whatever, Bro." Axel hung up abruptly.

Cam was bewildered for a few seconds. Why was he in such a snotty mood? *Whatever. Back at you, Bro.* He put his communication device on the nightstand and tried to clear his foggy mind. His brain was blank as he worked to recall why Axel would be bent out of shape. Ria's fingertips danced along his shoulders, sides and back, scratching, stroking and tenderly sliding across his skin, pulling him away from the mystery of the call and back to the primal feelings he had for the delicious female in his bed.

Cam needed more sleep to function at a hundred percent. At best, he was in the thirties.

He dimly remembered Axel's earlier call and heading out to meet him at the arrival lounge. Wait. One other shocking recollection struck harder, deeper and with more emotional force, waking him up better than any other incentive could.

Ria's picture—the one her mother had given him of her dressed richly in that cranberry suit—slammed into his mind. With instant, unwelcome clarity, Cam remembered his earlier foray out into the morning.

Axel's frantic call.

The cruise liner's missing passenger.

The visit with Director Patmore and Ria's mother.

The luscious picture of Ria dressed in the cranberry-colored suit.

He even remembered his immediate thought upon seeing it: *Good news. She's not an earthling.*

And then: *Bad news. She won't be spending the weekend after all.*

He'd hurried home to convince her to get back on the cruise liner so her mother and Director Patmore would be happy and the ship could make its moved-up departure time. He didn't want her to go, but knew he had to send her back. He hadn't sent her anywhere. He hadn't even mentioned it. Instead, he'd crawled back into bed to "snuggle" with her one last time.

He turned his head, opened his eyes and stared at Ria. She was also on her belly, wearing nothing but his shirt, eyes closed. The side of her head rested on one bent arm. Her other arm was stretched out, brushing the soft pads of her fingertips down his back.

The karaoke singer with the blue-streaked hair that he'd spent an extraordinary night—and morning—with was the missing passenger. An Alpha. In fact, she was a very wealthy, prestigious Alpha who was completely out of his league. He pushed out a long sigh as he realized she'd have to go back.

How had she ended up at the earthling karaoke bar? For whatever reason, he was grateful. For about two seconds. She'd broken one of the fundamental rules of the colony by leaving the way station and mingling with earthlings. She'd have to answer for it.

Space travelers aboard all ships from Alpha-Prime were strictly educated before arrival that the surrounding areas outside of Alienn were off limits without special permission obtained in advance. That special permission was always flagged on the manifests Cam received for arrivals. He well knew no passes had been authorized for the next several months. That meant Ria was a rogue passenger, loose on Earth. Based on the rules of the way station, he could shackle her and put her in the basement brig. All he had to do was slap the innocuous little strip he'd developed on her wrist and she would have no choice but to comply.

Cam stared at her beautiful, restful face. He tried to recapture the urgency he'd felt when he discovered the missing passenger was also the woman in his bed.

Her breathing deepened and she stopped stroking his back.

Ria the Rebellious was asleep again, curled on her side as if she didn't have a care in the world. He reached out to wake her, but stopped. He wasn't quite ready to let her go. He studied her face, the riotous blue streaks in her thick dark hair, and smiled as he wondered what her mother would think of the pop of color. She'd likely be livid.

Sensual exhaustion had forced them to recreate only a condensed version of the night before. Afterward, they'd both fallen asleep.

He hadn't mentioned he knew who she was. He had no regrets, but eventually she was going to have to go back to the cruise liner. When was it scheduled to leave? A couple of hours? He couldn't remember and his focus drifted again.

He pulled a stray lock of blue away from her cheek and tucked the strand behind her ear. She sighed. He moved closer, kissing her cheek. She was so soft, so sweet, so addictive. He kissed the corner of her mouth and she stirred. He brushed her lips with his in a light kiss meant to wake her gently. Then he did it again. The second time, she kissed him back.

Cam whispered, "Hey, you need to wake up." *But I hate to let you go.*

She cleared her throat and said softly, "I don't want to. Snuggle with me instead." The robust urge to do just as she said filled his body, but his mind told him to cool it. She needed to go back. Her mother was worried. Axel was upset. She'd broken the cardinal rule of travel to Earth, and maybe more than just the one. He could shackle her right now to force her cooperation. Hmm. That vision faded to a private place in his mind.

"Believe me, I want to snuggle with you more than anything, but you truly have to go back."

"Back? What do you mean? Back where? I want to stay here with you."

Cam hesitated. *I want you to stay here with me, too.* He forcefully shook off his desire. "I mean back to the spaceship. You weren't supposed to leave the basement facility without written permission. And you don't have either a note or a get-out-of-jail-free card."

Ria stiffened like her whole body had been zapped with lightning. Her eyes flew open and her lovely face looked stricken.

It was a bit embarrassing to realize he'd found her only by accident. He'd tried to read her thoughts last night and couldn't. That should have been a giant red flag. His ability to see into the minds of humans was greater than average. His inability to read her thoughts were because she was an Alpha and not because he'd had too much to drink. He should have realized. Security and watching out for trouble was his job, after all, even when he was off duty.

She cleared her throat and tried to brazen it out. "What makes you think I'm from—what did you call it?—a spaceship? Or that I don't have permission to go wherever I want?" She laughed as if a lack of permission to roam the wilds of Earth was the most ridiculous thing she'd ever heard.

"Because the call I got earlier was in reference to you. I had to go because I'm the chief security officer for the Big Bang Truck Stop way station here on Earth. A passenger was missing from the *Royal Caldera Forte*. Your mother showed me your picture.

"You, my sweet, rebellious Ria, are blatantly defying the rules of the way station by roaming off the grounds without prior permission. You especially were not authorized to be at that human karaoke bar. I have the authority to put you in the brig and shackle you if you resist."

Ria sat up. She couldn't have looked more horrified if she woke to find a crust-fish in bed with her. "Oh my gosh. You're an *Alpha*?"

"Yes. And so are you."

"How is that possible? You were in an earthling bar!" she said, her tone accusatory.

"So were you!" he accused right back. "Illegally, I might add. I live here. I can go where I want." His presence at the bar wasn't exactly sanctioned, but it wasn't against any rules. In theory.

Her gaze roamed his body for a few seconds. Under her breath, she said, "Of course you're built like an Alpha. You *are* one." She shook her head again. "How could I have been so fooled? Wait. What did you say about a brig and a shackle?"

"Never mind that for now." He wasn't planning on shackling her or putting her in jail. *Am I? No. Stop it.* "Why were you even off the ship in the first place?"

Ria's expression remained stunned. She stared like she hadn't seen him before and offered, "I was exploring?"

He huffed. "Oh? Illegally exploring, though, right?"

Her eyes narrowed and the rebellious smile that had snared his attention last night resurfaced. "But that's the best kind." Her head tilted to one side. "Do you do *everything* you're told to do?"

Cam didn't even have to think about it. "Yes. Of course."

She scanned him from hairline to chin and then from shoulders to knees. "I should have known you weren't an earthling."

Cam smiled at her defiant attitude. "Why is that?"

One shoulder lifted. "Well, besides your very Alpha build, I'm usually better at reading people." She tapped one side of her head with a knowing smile. The first thing Alphas learned about humans was their susceptibility to gentle mindreading and sometimes persuasion.

"Me, too," he admitted.

"Is that so?"

"Yep."

"And here I thought I'd had too much to drink.

Earthling alcoholic drinks are yummy and potent."

He nodded. "That's what I thought, too. I truly believed you were an earthling until this morning when I saw your picture."

"Really?" Her expression brightened and then just as quickly disappeared. "Or are you just saying that to be nice?"

Cam laughed. "Ask anyone, especially my siblings, and they'll tell you I'm rarely nice."

She moved closer. "Well, you're nice to me." She brushed her fingertips along his cheek and jaw.

"I like you."

"I like you, too." Her fingers glided down his neck to his shoulder, and she moved her soft, luscious body even closer. *Danger.*

She kissed his shoulder. She trailed a few more kisses along his skin and soon reached the base of his neck. She moved to straddle him, resting on her knees, and looked down into his eyes with a fierce expression.

"I don't want to go back. Not yet, anyway. Besides, I have a couple of days before anyone gets riled up about my absence, if they even notice I'm gone. Besides my mother, that is."

Oh, trust me. They noticed.

Ria put a light kiss on his lips. The feel of it reverberated all the way to his lonely soul. He didn't want her to go, either. But she had to get back on the cruise liner. It had to depart Earth soon.

Through the sensual haze her kisses produced without fail, he remembered the flight had been rescheduled to leave earlier than anticipated. Apparently she'd made her getaway before learning about the new curfew for the passengers. Typically, before sunup was the best time for ships to depart, but that wasn't an option due to the moved-up schedule. How much time did he have left to spend with her? *Whatever it is, it won't be enough.*

From his living room came an unexpected sound. *Bong. Bong. Bong.* It was his grandfather clock. He'd ordered it online all the way from Germany after saving up for months to get it delivered. The shipping charges alone had required nearly an Archetech's ransom.

Bong. Bong. Bong. The grandfather clock kept chiming. Cam had set it to peal only at noon and midnight. For the first time since waking, he noticed the bright beams of sunlight streaming into his bedroom from the thin space on either side not shielded by his curtains. That usually didn't happen until…

"Wait a minute. What time is it?" he asked the air around him. *Bong. Bong. Bong.*

Ria, still straddling his lap, pointed to the digital alarm clock on his nightstand and raised her voice to be heard over the grandfather clock's resonant chimes. "Twelve o'clock, right?"

"Noon?" The cruise liner was scheduled to leave at nine.

Ria wasn't on the ship. Had Axel said it already left? Cam couldn't understand all the tidbits of information jostling for attention in his head. The ship hadn't waited for her? How was that even possible?

Bong. Bong. Bong.

His grandfather clock finally struck the last chime. The eerie silence that followed echoed through his house.

Cam was awash in confusion. How could the ship not have waited for her to return?

Ria, sounding very concerned, asked, "What's wrong? You look disturbed."

"The *Royal Caldera Forte* departed Earth three hours ago."

Chapter 4

Ria laughed. "No, it didn't. It couldn't have. It's not scheduled to leave till after the weekend. Besides, they wouldn't leave without me. Would they?" Equal parts joy and despair vied for attention in her brain. "My mother would never leave me here all by myself. Trust me on this." Her forearms rested on his shoulders. She leaned in, relishing the close proximity of this perfect man. An Alpha, in fact. Perfect.

"Because she'd worry about you?"

Cam was so sweet to think that. "No, because she's got an agenda."

"An agenda?"

"I'm supposed to marry this dirt bag… I mean, a Technician's son. This trip was sort of a chance to get the families together prior to the public declaration of the pre-arranged marriage announcement.

"Except that his parents decided not to go at the last minute, supposedly to give us time alone—personally, I believe they don't care one whit about it either way—but my mother came along with us as a chaperone." She rolled her eyes. "As if I needed one with him." She sent him a scandalous look. "I didn't, by the way." She'd never even kissed Dirt Bag, let alone any of the delicious and wonderful things that had happened last night…and again this morning with Cam.

"Really?" His sexy half-smile made her weak.

"Yes. Really. From my perspective, we don't suit. At. All."

"Tell me more about this man you're supposed to marry."

"No. Not a good idea."

His brows curved up. "Why not?"

She shrugged. "Why do you need to know?"

That super desirable and now very familiar lopsided half-smile returned. "How else am I going to be able to compare myself to him and improve my chances?"

"I call him Dirt Bag FitzOsbern instead of Douglass Barnard FitzOsbern. What does that tell you?"

His smile deepened. "Ooh. Of the Elite Alpha-Prime Technician Class FitzOsberns, I presume?"

Ria stiffened and then scrambled off his lap. "How did you know *that*? Do you know them?"

That would be just her luck, to fall for a guy who was related to the dirt bag she was supposed to marry. Wouldn't that make all future family reunions interesting? She could practically hear her future mother-in-law say, "And here's our cousin

Cam. I understand Ria already knows him of course…in the biblical sense." She'd read that phrase and definition in a book on Earther culture when she couldn't wait to know an earthling "in the biblical sense." She thought she'd accomplished that last night—and this morning. However, Cam wasn't an earthling and now she didn't want anyone else. She mentally crossed out earthling on her Earth trip to-do list, wrote Earther, and then mentally crossed that out, too.

He shook his head. "I don't know them, but your mother mentioned it."

The fake future family reunion fantasy evaporated. "Of course she did. She's very proud to be nearly associated with the FitzOsbern family." She frowned. "Wait a minute. You spoke to her? My mother?"

Cam nodded as he moved to put some distance between them. He still sat on the bed, but with one leg bent at the knee and one foot on the floor. Ria leaned her back against the headboard to face him. They weren't touching, which she thought was a shame.

"Was she upset that I was missing?"

He nodded once more. "Come to think of it, she was also very concerned that Douglass Barnard FitzOsbern, a Technician's son, by the way, was beside himself with worry. But he didn't bother to leave the ship with your mother to look for you or express his concern in person."

Ria rolled her eyes. "I doubt he was the least alarmed about my whereabouts. He didn't pay much attention to me on the weeklong trip from Alpha-Prime to Earth. Without his parents present, he was even more horrible to me than usual and obviously not concerned about my mother's opinion, either."

"What did he do?"

"For starters, he made it clear he finds me a lesser candidate to take on the role of his wife. I'm not even in his class, you know. He then used that excuse to promptly ogle every female but me the entire time we were together. It's well known that when he's not in gaming halls, he's spending time with every woman he stumbles across. He's a total elitist, womanizing jerk. I'm better off without him."

Cam narrowed his eyes. "Elitist, womanizing jerk?"

"Isn't that the right Earther phrase?"

"Yes. And it's inventive. How do you know it?"

Ria settled back against his padded headboard. "I studied up on Earth before making this trip." Thanks to the little-known book of phrases and Earther meanings she'd tucked away for the trip.

"So…elitist, womanizing jerks, escaping a cruise liner without being caught and operational awareness of karaoke bars? What interesting study material you found for your journey."

She laughed. "I read a great many things about Earth before I even got on the ship."

"Was 'How to Get an Earthling Into Bed' one of your homework topics?"

She sobered and stared at him intently, willing him to believe it when she said, "Not exactly. It's a good thing, too, since you aren't an earthling."

"You didn't know that until now."

"True, but I've also never felt about another the way I feel about you, whether Alpha or earthling, or Earther. I was drawn to you. There's something about you—and only you—that makes me—" she paused, trying to find the right word. "Yearn. I yearn to know you better. You engage me. The moment I saw you, I wanted to talk to you. I wanted to learn everything about you." She grinned. "I wanted to sing to you."

"You did sing to me," he said, his tone low and raspy.

Ria leaned up from the headboard, moving closer. "Because I wanted you so much. And I didn't stop myself from approaching you, like I would have back home. I thought you were an earthling. Someone I'd never see again, and that helped kill any remaining resistance." She slung an arm around his neck, but he didn't move.

She backed off a bit. "What's up?"

"I need to leave." He glanced at his phone before his gaze settled back on her.

"Can I go with you?"

His brows furrowed. "Not yet."

She expelled a long sigh. "Okay, then can I

scrounge around in your kitchen for food?"

He paused for a few seconds, as if he wasn't used to having anyone in his house or making use of his things. "Sure. Go ahead."

"Do you have any coffee, by chance?" She'd learned in her studies that many Alphas thought coffee on Earth was better than what got shipped to Alpha-Prime.

He laughed. "Yes. I have a machine that makes one cup at a time so you can try some different flavors if you want."

"Excellent. Thank you."

He kissed her quickly on the mouth, then stood up before she could respond. Without looking at her, he grabbed pieces of clothing he'd dropped to the floor this morning and put them on, covering up his beautiful, perfect body.

"You will be back, won't you?" She tried not to sound needy and desperate, even though that was her current train of thought.

"Of course."

"So you're not finished with me yet?"

He paused at the bedroom door, his expression troubled. "You heard that, huh?"

She nodded.

"I don't want to be, but I probably should be."

"Why?"

He cleared his throat. "Technically, you're spoken for."

She shrugged. "Not really. No announcement

has been made. No papers have been signed. I'm free. For now."

He tilted his head as if he didn't buy it. "Still. Eventually papers will be signed and ultimately an announcement will be made. Right?"

She shrugged. "In this moment, I truly wish those things won't ever happen. I don't want them to happen. If I had the power to stop them, I would in an instant. Unfortunately, my mother is in love with Dirt Bag's elite lineage. She's going to be hard to convince otherwise. I'm not certain I have the final say."

"Yeah. She seemed pretty proud of the coming union."

"Oh, she is, trust me. The elder FitzOsberns seem fairly indifferent. He's the fourth of four sons, and not even an heir to the lion's share of their wealth. His three older brothers run their family business, while he only has a title on the board of directors." She shrugged. "My opinion is that they just want the arranged marriage over and done with so their youngest can finally move out of their house."

"What does he do for work? Or is a title on the board his only job?"

"That's right. He does nothing in the way of work. He socializes in the Elite circles where he doesn't have to do anything to earn money. Even a fourth of what he'll inherit is enough to live on until his death and then some, unless he goes crazy with it."

"Sounds boring."

"I know, right? My mother, however, is from a different era. She wants a 'good' marriage for me so I'll be provided for the rest of my life. And because of some careful wording in the arranged marriage agreement signed when I was a baby, my mother will also be kept in the manner she's accustomed to. My marriage to Dirt Bag takes care of her for life."

"And your father? What did he think about this arranged marriage agreement?"

She shook her head. "He died several years ago, leaving nothing for me to inherit, and therefore no funds for my mother to live comfortably on for the rest of her days. Hence, her big push for this arranged marriage."

"I'm sorry about your father." The sorrowful look he sent her way was sincere.

"Me, too. I miss him. He was always the buffer between me and my mother."

"No siblings?"

"Nope, just me. What about you? How many siblings do you have?"

Cam's eyebrows rose. "Lots. I have a large family."

"How large?"

"Seven kids."

"Really? All boys?"

"Six boys and one girl."

A smile shaped her lips. "I'll bet it was fun growing up in your house."

"If you ask my mother, it was lively, that's for certain." He looked at the bedside clock. "I need to check who got on the cruise liner, since it obviously wasn't you."

She pushed out a long sigh and nodded. She should likely be concerned that the ship had left without her, but all she felt was total and utter relief. How long before her mother sought her out in her suite and found she wasn't on board? Would she demand they turn the ship around? Would the captain do it and jeopardize everyone's vacation plans because Ria had managed to miss the boat, literally?

If Dirt Bag discovered she'd stayed behind on Earth, would he even care? Or would he simply continue gawking at other women and flirting without her there to see him do it and try to lure them into bed since she wasn't there to see him do that, either?

Ria didn't have to think hard about the answer to that question. He might not have noticed her at all if her mother wasn't there to constantly shove Ria directly into his personal space. It seemed as much as Ria didn't want to marry him, her dirt bag intended didn't want to marry her either.

Before departing Alpha-Prime, she'd overheard him tell one of his friends the pending wedding announcement and get-to-know-your-future-bride journey wouldn't change much about the way he operated. He planned to do whatever he wanted up to the day he was chained in matrimony to a bride who was so much lower down the ladder from his own lofty place in Elite Alpha-Prime society. He didn't like being forced into an arranged marriage, she'd heard him tell his friend. Therefore, he didn't need to be true to the woman he married.

Dirt Bag was an enthusiastic snob, another Earther term she'd assigned him in her mind. The Earther term gold digger was likely the best way to describe how he thought about her. On Alpha-Prime, a rank rambler was someone on the prowl to increase their standing in the social stratosphere of Alpha-Prime.

Ria liked gold digger better. If a nasty term was going to be used to label her, she preferred the Earther one. The term rank rambler sent a shameful burning sensation directly into her chest every time she heard it.

"Hurry back," she told Cam.

Ria's new plan included another term she'd learned from her Earther reference book. Elopement.

Would Cam be willing to run away with her and let her stay on Earth?

Chapter 5

Cam knew he should go, but walked back to the bed, leaned down and kissed Ria's mouth briefly. She seemed deep in thought until he kissed her. Any more engaging lip locks would result in too much time going by. He needed to leave. He needed to see if the cruise liner had departed and how it managed to leave without Ria.

He tried to stay on his original train of thought, but every kiss, touch, and look sidetracked him. Ria was like a drug in his system, a dangerous one. He was grateful she wasn't enamored of the man she was supposed to marry. Not that it would change anything. Arranged marriages were difficult to escape or dismiss unless both parties agreed to sever the agreement.

Having met her mother, Cam knew the Governess would never willingly give up a Technician's son in favor of a colony outpost security man, as she'd sneeringly called him.

Ria smiled, slid gracefully out of his bed and stretched like a feline after a long afternoon nap.

His shirt definitely looked better on her.

"I'll be back shortly," Cam said and hurried out before he stayed and lost total track of time. Again. He hopped into his small SUV and drove the short distance to the Big Bang Truck Stop for the second time that day.

He passed Aunt Dixie's home and resisted the urge to whisper an incantation to ward off evil spirits as he drove by. Cam shook his head, remembering the day she moved in. His aunt spent quite a lot of time working on schemes to earn money for an old folks' home, a place she didn't actually live most of the time.

Having his very eccentric aunt reside only a few doors down was always interesting. She'd been known to drop by unannounced. He figured she wanted to catch him with a girl and grill him about his marriage intentions. She'd spent a month raving to Diesel about free milk and cows when his older brother started dating Juliana.

Mostly, Cam managed to avoid being the target of her wacky schemes. That didn't mean it was out of the realm of possibility.

Aunt Dixie spent the bulk of her time haranguing his eldest brother Diesel, in his capacity as Fearless Leader and manager of the Big Bang Truck Stop, to approve her never-ending and completely outlandish ideas to make money for the old folks' home. A recent one involved a wet T-shirt contest at the home using Big Bang Truck

Stop T-shirts. Aunt Dixie insisted it would be good advertising for the upstairs side of the business.

Diesel put the brakes on that plan.

A month before that, she'd wanted to produce a very candid silver fox calendar and had already lined up twelve elderly volunteers to "drop trou," as she put it, to "rake in the big bucks." Diesel quashed that plan seconds after hearing it.

Cam felt sorry for his brother, but didn't want to inherit the job of keeping Aunt Dixie in line if Diesel decided to run screaming from her seemingly endless schemes.

He parked his SUV in the truck stop's side lot. He'd once helped carry Diesel's Earther girlfriend, Juliana, to her car after shooting her with a Defender to make her forget about seeing a Moogalian alien on the loose in the side lot. At the time, they'd thought she was pure human, and had just witnessed the drunken half-sea creature, half-humanoid attempt to enter a forbidden door to the basement facility.

Diesel had been rather perturbed, but Cam had just been doing his job as chief of security. He smiled at the memory, but quickly frowned as he thought about Ria being zapped and forgetting things about their time together.

She was an Alpha, which meant the Defender wouldn't work on her. It was a great tool to keep earthlings from finding out about what really went on at the Big Bang Truck Stop's basement facility. He realized now he had a better understanding of his big brother's supreme frustration with him over the matter back then, even though it was the right call. He was also lucky Juliana forgave him.

Last night, he'd contemplated the possible need to use the device on Ria if she found out about his alien identity, but hoped it would never come to that. Well, now it never *would* come to that. Alphas were immune to the effects of the Defender and his Ria was a beautiful, free-spirited Alpha…and very nearly promised forever to another man.

He frowned and tried to think of something other than dwelling on her possible future with someone else.

Cam wasn't certain he wanted to talk to Axel just yet. Would Diesel know about the cruise liner and what had happened? Surely he would. With his quick plan in place, he raced downstairs and headed toward his office to discuss the matter with someone—anyone—other than Axel.

Diesel spotted him before he made it to the sanctuary of his office and waved him over. As Cam approached, one of three women from the recovery team dispatched last month to Nocturne Falls, appeared from the basement entrance right next to Diesel.

"Elise Greene, as I live and breathe," Diesel said. "How are you doing after your adventures in Georgia?" Elise's gaze cut to Cam, her boss, as if she wasn't certain how to answer. Cam knew exactly why.

"Diesel, what's wrong with you? Her last name is Midori, not Greene. Victoria's last name is Greene."

His brother frowned, turning to Elise for confirmation. She looked sheepish and said, "That's right. Midori, not Greene."

"Wait a minute. How long have I had your name wrong?" Diesel's horrified expression as he asked the question was likely answer enough.

Cam chose not to let it go. His team member deserved his support. "Well, gee, Diesel. How long did you think her name was Greene and not Midori?"

Elise Midori, Victoria Greene and their cousin Stella Grey had been dispatched after a UFO from Alpha-Prime crashed near Nocturne Falls on its way to Alienn, Arkansas's underground way station. Their mission had been to retrieve the pilot, guard and prisoner on the transport, and conceal the existence of extraterrestrials on Earth. They'd found a lot more than they bargained for, but that was a story for another day.

His brother shrugged. "Well, I guess…since she's worked here." He looked confused and dismayed over his mistake. "But Midori means green, doesn't it, in Italian?"

"And yet her name remains Midori and not Greene in whatever language you choose."

Elise smiled indulgently. "Honestly, I don't think you've ever called me by the wrong last name before. Usually, you just say, 'Hey there, Elise' and move on."

Diesel pushed out a sigh. "Well, I'm sorry I've had it wrong in my head all this time, but—"

Cam broke in. "Wait for it, Elise, he's about to play the 'I'm a lovesick dude' card because he's got a woman in his life."

"Bite me, Cam," Diesel said with a grin. To Elise he said, "Again, my apologies for the error and, yes, I'm also a lovesick dude, by way of explanation."

"I accept your apology even though it isn't needed, and I hope you aren't further thrown off when I tell you that my last name isn't Midori anymore."

"It's not?"

Cam narrowed his gaze. "You changed your name? Really?"

"Well, it's not common knowledge yet, but Riker and I eloped. We wanted to have a ceremony in Alienn with Riker's brother Draeken before we head back to Alpha-Prime."

Diesel and Cam both said at the same time, "You married The Calderian? Awesome!" The Calderian was Alpha-Prime's top law enforcement entity. Riker Phoenix was just as well known on Earth as on their home planet.

Cam and Diesel looked at each other and said,

"Jinx! You owe me a soda." They also punched each other in the shoulder.

Elise laughed. "Thanks. I think he's awesome, too."

Diesel said in a low, urgent tone, "Okay. Elise Phoenix. Elise Phoenix. Elise Phoenix. Maybe if I keep chanting it, I'll remember."

"Good luck with that, old timer," Cam said. "Elise, I'm sorry to lose such a good operative, but you have my sincere congratulations. When do you leave?"

"Well, I can stay until things are sorted in the roster. I certainly don't want to leave you in a bind—"

Cam stopped her with an upheld hand. "I'm sure The Calderian is needed back on Alpha-Prime, and that you're both eager to start your lives there together. Let me worry about the schedule. I'll also make sure you have glowing references from me and our Fearless Leader here to take with you."

Her cheeks colored and her eyes glistened with emotion. "Thanks, Cam. That means a lot to me."

"Like I said, you'll be missed. With your experience, you won't have any trouble finding a suitable position on Alpha-Prime." Uncomfortable, Cam looked at Diesel. "Now, back to why I'm even here on my day off. Have you seen Axel today?"

Diesel said, "Nope." Elise shook her head.

So far, so good. "Did you know that the *Royal Caldera Forte* had to leave early?"

"Yep. I saw the memo. Something about a volcanic ash plume in space on the scheduled route, right?"

Cam nodded.

"Do I win something?" Diesel's expression suddenly sobered. "Wait a minute. You took a day off? When a ship was docked in Alienn? What's the matter with you?"

"Bite me, Diesel." He expected his brother to mention something about the missing passenger, but he didn't. "Axel had it covered." *Sort of, until he called me about the missing passenger and then the ship left without her.*

Did Diesel know a passenger had been missing? Better not find out right now. He'd suck it up and speak to a hostile Axel before admitting anything like that to his eldest brother. A meeting of the council of elders might be called and a judgment rendered. And if anyone there found out where the missing passenger was—rustling up breakfast in Cam's kitchen after spending the better part of a night and morning rolling around with him in bed—or that an imposter was now aboard the ship, he wasn't certain what would happen.

Now he was back to discussing this matter with Axel. Diesel would give him a further rash of grief if he admitted to sleeping with or actively hiding the missing passenger.

He left Diesel, who laughed at him openly. Elise at least had good manners. She tried not to smile behind the fingers over her mouth, but her eyes were amused. Cam headed toward Axel's office with the intention of leaving a note for his brother to call him. No such luck. He ran into Axel right outside his office door.

Axel's eyes widened in surprise, but he snorted. "What are you doing here? I thought your sacred time off would keep you at home." His brother was obviously holding a grudge. Cam sighed deeply and bore up to deal with this issue.

"Very funny. I was so exhausted that I went to bed and conked out the moment I got home." Axel didn't have to know what happened *before* he fell asleep. "I swear, I was only going to rest for a minute...and then you called and I wasn't awake enough for a second conversation, either."

"Oh?" Axel seemed to understand he wasn't getting the whole story, but didn't press. "What are you doing here now?"

Cam cleared his throat. "I'm here because of your earlier phone call." This would be a good time to make nice with his brother. He did owe him.

"What about it?"

Cam rolled his shoulders to help relax his stiff posture. "I regret not helping you find the passenger."

Axel crossed his arms and leaned a shoulder against the doorframe. "Really? You have regrets?"

"Yes. Really. I get it. You were doing me a favor by taking care of this situation even though it's my day off. I should have been more considerate instead of going home to...take a much needed nap." *Eventually.*

"Who are you? And what have you done with my brother, Cam?"

"Very funny."

"Is this your way of saying you're sorry?"

He shrugged. "Maybe."

Axel grinned. "Okay. I graciously accept your thoughtful, totally sincere and totally regret-filled apology."

"Don't get crazy now." Axel laughed and Cam knew he was forgiven. "So, tell me what happened with the missing passenger."

Axel tilted his head to one side, like a dog trying to understand what its human was saying. "I told you already. She walked onto the ship through the Elite passenger door and, moments later, the cruise liner left the dock. Boom. Ka-pow." He clapped his hands together once and then made a gesture like something taking off into the wild blue yonder. "They even made it five minutes ahead of schedule, which must have pleased Director Patmore to no end."

Cam didn't have a good feeling about this. "So you personally saw her get aboard?"

"Yes. I saw her board the ship myself. Why? What's wrong?"

Cam couldn't very well tell him the truth...exactly. At least not yet.

"Nothing's wrong. You sounded irritated when you called. I wanted to make sure nothing else was going on beyond me not helping with the search." Cam knew precisely why his brother had been angry.

Axel's eyes narrowed. "You left and went home and purposely didn't look for the missing passenger. So, yeah, I'll admit I was a little annoyed. But now you've said you're woefully sorry, that you simply couldn't go another second without my forgiveness and you'll never, ever leave me hanging out to dry again. I have accepted your courteous regrets even though you didn't really have a good reason not to help me."

Cam repeated what was likely the lamest excuse in the world. "Well, I was really tired."

"From what, having a day off?"

Cam shrugged. "Well. Yeah. Maybe I went out and partied and then came home late last night." He'd been exhausted from staying up all night with Ria.

"Oh? You partied all night? What's her name?"

Cam managed a quick, "No comment."

"That means you *were* with someone."

"It *was* my day off." Without admitting he was with a woman and especially not saying her nickname or who she really was, he said, "Let's just say I didn't turn in early last night expecting to go to work this morning. Your call was unforeseen."

Axel shrugged. "Are you saying that it was my

fault you didn't look for the missing passenger when you knew it was only the two of us out there searching?"

Cam put his hands up in surrender. "No. That's not what I said. I just wondered what happened and where you found her."

"Why? What difference does it make?"

"Maybe I'll add it to the watch list under where to look for escaped aliens off recently docked cruise liners at the way station. I know you were annoyed you had to look for her all by yourself. But can you get over it long enough to tell me where you found her? I just wondered where she was hiding out." *To ensure no one looks at my house.*

It was Axel's turn to look sheepish. "I didn't find her. She came in of her own accord."

Cam frowned. Someone came in, but not Ria. Who was it? "Explain."

"Well, she came in with her lady's maid," Axel amended.

"She had a maid? I didn't hear about that. So there were two Alphas loose in town this morning?" He threw his hands in the air as if truly put out, but wasn't.

"Not exactly. You see, after her mother talked to us and was apparently unimpressed with what she called the 'lackluster security systems' in place on this backwater colony, she sent their personal lady's maid out to help look for Alexandria. I got back from *my* useless search just in time to learn about the lady's maid and then see the missing passenger return with the maid following dutifully along behind."

"Where did this Alexandria say she'd been?"

"She didn't," Axel said. "At least not to me. I saw her board the ship through the Elite Class door along with her lady's maid. Director Patmore also watched them climb aboard. He was the one who allowed the maid to go off on her own to find her. Once the two returned, he signed the manifest confirming he had a complete roster of passengers, gave me a copy and away they went."

"Huh. Interesting."

"Is it? What's so interesting?"

A question Cam couldn't answer. He didn't know who'd gotten on the ship, but it wasn't Ria. "I don't know. That her maid brought her back, I guess. How did she know where to look? Why wasn't she present during our meeting with her mother? Why did we have to look for her if her lady's maid was going to be dispatched to find her right away? And it had to be somewhere in the facility, right? Otherwise, the maid would've had to leave the vicinity, which she most definitely didn't have permission to do."

Axel nodded, his expression shifting to one of resolve. "Good point. You're probably right. The lady's maid likely knew exactly where the girl was the whole time and simply fetched her."

"Maybe," Cam murmured, knowing that wasn't

the truth at all. But if the lady's maid did go somewhere, who came back with her? *Please, please don't let it be some stray earthling you picked up along the side of the road.*

The calamitous possibility of earthling exposure to aliens flying around the galaxy on a cruise liner not scheduled to return for ten days flitted through his mind. Cam's heart skipped a beat. *What can I do? What should I do?*

Maybe Cam should get a carefully worded message ready to send to the ship, warning the crew to be on the lookout for any wide-eyed earthlings found aboard ogling all the aliens. Then again, if it wasn't an earthling, he didn't want to stir up trouble.

Cam noticed Axel's rare serious expression and stopped his mental speculation.

"What is wrong with you, Bro?" Axel asked.

He shrugged. "I don't know what you mean." He turned to go.

"Your tense face alone could worry the horns off a billy goat."

Cam rolled his eyes. He was not tense. He was the exact opposite after spending the night with Ria. "No. Wrong. I'm not tense, just tired. You called me out of a sound sleep on my day off to look for someone who came back on her own without me being involved at all. If you'd never called me, I'd likely still be asleep. I should be the one perturbed, not you."

"Oh, a thousand pardons for disturbing you, my liege," Axel said with extra sarcasm. "Next time there's a problem, I'll let chaos run rampant before disturbing your beauty sleep. I can see you need every second. Your attitude is fairly crappy when you don't get enough shut-eye."

"Funny." Cam blew out a short breath. "Keep in mind I'll also remember this the next time *you* have a day off."

"Whatever. Go. I promise I won't bother you again."

"Thanks. Much appreciated." Cam walked away with several thoughts zipping through his head. The only one worth worrying about was whether an earthling was aboard the *Royal Caldera Forte*. The ship would return in ten days. No matter how much he wanted it to, his invention wouldn't be able to wipe that much time from an earthling's memory. The max range of a Defender was thirty minutes. He'd have to employ an older method of removing the earthling's memories.

Once the ship returned to Earth, he'd simply corner the impersonator and ensure she got either a mega zap from an experimental deluxe Defender that erased several days' worth of memories, or they'd have to use the memory serum and a hypodermic needle to ensure no memories of the trip through space remained in the human's brain.

Cam's overriding concern had more to do with how many others might discover an earthling had been loose on an alien ship for ten days, while the way station's security chief entertained an AWOL Alpha without alerting anyone.

That would set off a space potato storm of epic proportions.

Chapter 6

Cam left the basement facility more confused and definitely more concerned than he'd been upon his entrance. He didn't know who'd boarded the ship, but it wasn't Ria. The ship would return in ten days. The only true concern was whether the imposter was an Alpha or an earthling.

After only a few minutes of thought, he dismissed the idea of sending a formal message to the ship. He couldn't trust it would only be read by the onboard law enforcement officer. There was a real danger it would be leaked or read by the entire ship during the course of the trip.

Wide knowledge of an imposter would likely end up biting him in the butt if he admitted knowledge about the phony passenger aboard at this early stage. If a horrific issue with an earthling aboard developed, he'd hear about it before much longer.

He mulled over what problems he'd have to deal with if he waited for the ship's return without sending a heads up in advance. If the fake passenger was quiet about her excursion and behaved with the goal of simply wanting to enjoy a deluxe vacation, he might not have to admit anything. Calling attention to the mix-up now might open a can of worms he'd just as soon stayed closed.

If this had happened to Axel, he probably wouldn't worry about it at all. His carefree brother would skip to work singing Zip-a-Dee-Doo-Dah, smile through every worrisome difficulty and sleep like a coma patient. Maybe Cam would try Axel's carefree-lifestyle for the next ten days and see what happened. He'd keep his ear to the ground for any communications, messages or issues from the ship, and hope the notion of out of sight, out of mind might work in this situation.

He wasn't going to lie. As much angst as this caused one part of his mind, another part was wildly elated. With an imposter on board and no one actively looking for Ria, it meant he'd have her to himself for the next ten days. Another part of him was troubled when he remembered the future fiancé aboard the ship. It sounded like she'd be better off without him. If the guy looked at other women and couldn't see how perfect Ria was, he was an idiot.

Because one look at Ria had Cam besotted beyond all reason.

Was her future fiancé blind or simply a rich, elitist, womanizing, jerk, dirt bag as she'd stated?

While they hadn't formalized their arranged

marriage agreement, Ria didn't seem as excited about the prospect of marrying a Technician's son as her mother was. Still, perhaps Cam should tread carefully while they were together. Maybe he shouldn't spend the next week and a half in bed with her, as much as that thought appealed.

Maybe they could just spend the time hanging out like very good friends, getting to know each other. He could show her Earth and all the things he loved about it. That would be fun. Seeing his life-long home through the eyes of someone from Alpha-Prime would be interesting. Up to now, he'd only dated earthlings. Perhaps he'd subconsciously waited for Ria. Too bad she was spoken for.

He shook off the melancholy and retrieved his new happy-go-lucky attitude, the one he would copy from Axel.

Alphas typically fell into two camps with regard to sightseeing on this planet. They either loved Earth because it was so different from Alpha-Prime or hated it for the exact same reason. The one thing everyone remarked on was the tall trees.

There was one other risk he'd have to keep in mind. If he squired Ria around town, he'd have to be careful not to let Axel see her. He'd recognize her almost instantly. If anyone else saw them together, Cam would simply say she was an earthling he was seeing. Wouldn't Diesel love that, given all the times Cam had neutralized Juliana's memories when they started dating?

Okay, maybe he'd avoid both Axel and Diesel for the next ten days.

The other thing he needed to do was extend his long weekend into a full-fledged ten-day vacation. That stunning news, and the resulting shift in workload to cover for him, might keep both Axel and Diesel too busy at the Big Bang Truck Stop to keep track of what Cam was doing. That would free him to spend as much quality time as he could with Ria until she had to leave.

The mere idea of never seeing Ria again or, worse, thinking of her forever linked with the guy she called Dirt Bag FitzOsbern, raised his fury to a level he'd never before experienced. He didn't like it. Not the manic feeling or the thought of her being forever attached to some other guy.

Taking a deep breath, Cam calmed himself, promising to live in the moment or rather to live in the next ten days, soaking up as much time with her as he could. He'd decide what to do about the imposter when the ship returned, and vowed not to worry over that which he didn't have control anyway.

Cam returned home to find Ria in the kitchen instead of his bedroom. It was a good start to his new stay-out-of-bed plan.

She stood at the breakfast bar sipping what looked like coffee. She looked so beautiful in his shirt, his breath hitched for a second before he entered the room.

Ten days alone with her would be both heaven and hell, but he wouldn't miss it for anything. "Ria." Her name caressed his lips as he said it.

"Cam." She took another sip of coffee and saluted him with her steaming cup. "You have really wonderful coffee here."

"Better than what you get on Alpha-Prime?"

"Oh, yes. It tastes richer somehow and there are flavors I've never heard of before." She sighed and sipped more. "This one is pumpkin spice. Also, I had something with blueberry in the name."

"You've already had two cups? I didn't think I'd been gone long enough."

She giggled. "Actually, this is my third cup since you've been gone. I started with something called Rainforest Reserve and, honestly, they are all my favorites."

"Good. I'm glad you like the variety." Cam moved to her side and kissed her cheek. Before he could make a coffee for himself, she put her cup down on the counter, turned and kissed him hard on the mouth.

He responded in kind and with enthusiasm for the first thirty seconds, until he remembered her looming arranged marriage and her future fiancé, and broke the kiss, stepping away.

"What's wrong?" Her lips were delightfully puffy from their ardent lip lock.

"We probably need to stop doing that." He turned away to grab a mug from a low shelf and started making a cup of coffee, focusing with laser-like precision on his task, as if it was the most important beverage he'd ever make. He didn't want to say out loud the restriction he'd put on himself for the rest of their time together. Once he told her of his vow not to fall into bed with her again, he'd honor it.

"Why?" she asked in a small voice.

"You know why," he said softly, turning to show her his resolve.

She stared briefly, then looked away, grabbed her cup and took a deep drink of her steamy beverage. "Because of the arranged marriage, right?"

"Yes. I didn't know before, but now that I do, the honorable thing is to stop kissing you like I have a right to."

Ria nodded. "I understand. Maybe you're right. I don't like it, of course. But I get it. You're very nice."

"Seriously, I'm not that nice." He made his cup of coffee and they didn't say anything else about being nice or kissing or the lack of same that was about to be his reality.

Cam changed the subject. "Do you know anyone living here on Earth?"

She shrugged and a mischievous smile shaped her lovely lips. "I know you."

"I meant before you got here. Was there someone you'd planned to visit after your foray into the karaoke bar? Someone you'd planned to stay with or anything?"

"Nope. I didn't know a soul before now." She sent a heated gaze his way before she took another deep sip of coffee. "This is the first time I've been here. Even coming to Earth on the ship was a necessary evil, according to my mother. She would never allow me to befriend anyone on a colony planet, before or now. She's rather snobbish about what I consider our dubious high status. She and Dirt Bag have that in common."

"Dubious? What does that mean?"

"It means the only reason she is so zealous about having me accept the arranged marriage into this particular Technician family is because she's broke. My father didn't leave her as much money as she expected, given the status he managed to obtain. Certainly not enough funds for her to live the expensive cultured life she'd planned. After he was gone, she was certain he gambled all our money away or somehow foolishly lost the bulk of it before he died."

"Did he?"

She shrugged again. "I don't know. I wouldn't have thought so, but he did have a rebellious streak that he only showed on occasion."

"Guess you came by yours honestly, then."

"Guess so. Anyway, *that* is why my mother is much more excited about this arranged marriage than I am. Basically, I'm being traded away for money."

"What money?"

She let out a long sigh of frustration. "Included in this ancient marriage arrangement is a provision for the groom's family to not only pay for the probably elaborate wedding ceremony, but also to make a substantial financial payment to the bride's family once the nuptials are completed. Like a bride price. It's not a common practice, but it's a contracted part of this particular arranged marriage."

"Why, I wonder."

She lifted one shoulder, her expression scornful. "Maybe because he was the fourth son and his parents and family wanted to ensure he moved out one day. Or more likely because we were of a lower class, but a stand-up family and that was how it worked all those years ago. I'm not sure about that either, but I do know my mother is counting on those post-wedding funds to let her live her life the way she thinks befits her station, as the widow of a Governor." An exaggerated eye roll came with that assessment.

Cam took his mug from the brewer and inhaled the scent of his favorite coffee. Rainforest Reserve was the thickest, darkest, richest coffee he'd found. It never failed to jumpstart the mornings when he suffered from lack of sleep. After a sip or two, he was more alert, but Ria seemed to have a calming effect on him. He'd love nothing more than to curl up with her anywhere and simply sleep until tomorrow morning.

Another sip of powerful coffee brought with it a relevant thought. "What about your lady's maid?"

"Prudence? What about her? I assume you know about her from my mother."

He didn't correct her. "Does Prudence have any family on Earth?"

Ria nodded. "She has an aunt and a cousin or maybe two cousins. I'm not certain and I can't remember their names or anything. Why?"

Inside, he breathed a huge sigh of relief. At least the imposter was an Alpha, not a wayward earthling. "Your mother sent Prudence to look for you. She came back with someone pretending to be you. It sounds like maybe she just co-opted a vacation for one of her relatives."

Ria's eyes narrowed. "That doesn't sound like something Prudence would do. Perhaps her aunt or cousins talked her into something. I'd believe that more easily than any deception from Prudence, who, let's be clear, is really my mother's maid, not mine."

"Did Prudence know about your escape plans or where you might go on Earth?"

"No. She probably guessed that I wanted to visit some places on Earth besides the way station. And she also knew I wasn't allowed to go anywhere once we docked, but she certainly didn't know about my escape plans, the karaoke bar or that I'd end up with you."

He grinned. He couldn't seem to help it.

"I mean, *I* didn't even know I'd end up here in your house, so how could she?"

"My singular concern is whether she'd bring an earthling aboard the ship to pretend the woman was you."

Ria's eyes widened. "Oh. No. Prudence would never do that. If she brought someone onto the ship—and that's a big 'if'—then it was one of her Alpha relatives living here on Earth."

Cam allowed his shoulders to lower a fraction of an inch. "Well, that's something anyway. I won't have to do an extreme memory wipe on some unwitting human when the ship gets back in ten days. Or explain how I knew a human was aboard, but didn't mention it or try to warn anyone on the ship."

"You aren't going to do a memory wipe on me, are you? I don't want to forget you."

"The Defender I developed doesn't work on Alphas. Besides, we only wipe the memories of earthlings who find out about aliens living here in plain sight."

"You developed the Defender? I've heard of it."

He gave a self-conscious nod. "I like to tinker with things."

"Well, color me impressed," she said. "From what I understand, that's some pretty impressive technology. I'm certain you've invented other things to keep not only earthlings in line, but to keep rebellious Alphas like me from doing things we aren't supposed to."

The shackle sticker's subduing impact on Alphas drifted into his mind and he smacked it right out again. Shackling her was equal to a blinking red warning sign of unbelievable temptation. She'd be cooperative to the nth degree. She wouldn't resist any suggestion he made. Yes, dangerous with a capital D.

Not that she'd been less than compliant with any suggestions he'd made to this point. Besides, the shackle sticker inspired the kind of loss of will that was anything but enticing to him. No, what he liked was the idea of Ria submitting totally to him. Willingly.

He swallowed, hard, and reminded himself of his vow.

"Like sneak off a ship and allow an imposter to get on that same vehicle so you can play around on Earth for ten days?" He stared into her luscious hazel eyes.

She stared back. "Yes. Like that."

They watched each other rather intensely for several moments. He didn't dare move in her direction. After a few seconds, it seemed she planned to stay across the room, too.

Finally, he broke the silence. "I wouldn't use anything on you, Ria, even if I had it. Honestly, I don't want you to forget me." Why did simply staring at her beautiful face make his brain go so soft that he'd admit something volatile like that out loud? He should consider the shackle sticker an option. If this were anyone else, he already would have slapped one in place and led the renegade alien back to the basement brig for safekeeping until the ship returned.

But he couldn't do that to Ria. He didn't *want* to do it to her. And if anyone found out what he'd already let her get away with, it might cost him his job. Ria was worth it. And if she had to be here on Earth for the next ten days, who better to watch over her than the chief of security for the Big Bang Truck Stop?

His argument was as convenient as it was accurate. He was the person best qualified to keep an eye on her, if he also ignored the protocol for an escaped Alpha on the loose in Alienn without prior permission to explore.

The next ten days were going to test every one of the boundaries he'd put in place for himself. He always held himself to a higher standard. He always did the right thing. He never bent the rules to allow anyone or anything to endanger the secret about aliens living in plain sight on Earth, let alone sever them cleanly like he was now by not announcing to anyone what she'd done and shielding her unauthorized actions.

He glanced her way and his eyes caught on the sight of her rebellious blue-streaked hair as she sipped her coffee, sighing in simple pleasure. She was a sight to behold even though he knew her wicked ways.

Ria could tempt a saint to misbehave, but Cam was no saint.

Chapter 7

Ria wondered what Cam was thinking. He was attractive and appealing, and she would love nothing more than spending the next ten days testing the strength of his bedsprings. However, she wondered if they'd ever sleep together again. It wasn't a lack of desire on either of their parts, but he was trying to do the right thing.

She appreciated his honorable approach with regard to the foolish arranged marriage she was saddled with, and promised herself she'd do her best not to tempt him if he didn't want to be with her again.

It would be difficult, but she'd make the effort. And she did want to explore Earth and all the variety it had to offer. If she could spend the time with Cam while she did it, getting to know him, then that was even better. Besides, perhaps she could persuade him into an innocent kiss or two or a dozen along the way.

"I'm glad you don't want to forget me," he said.

"No matter what happens, I swear I'll never forget you."

After a lengthy silence, she asked, "So, let's say I want to explore the area. Where will you take me? Or are you putting me in the brig, shackled and waiting for the ship to return?"

"While putting you behind bars or in a shackle is tempting and likely what I *should* do, I'll let you roam free with the understanding that when the ship returns, you must go back and follow the rules."

She nodded, but wondered if she could ever go back to following *any* rules. She hated rules. Rules were dumb. Ancient rules and practices from her planet were the reason she was even in an arranged marriage in the first place. But sometimes even the mighty oak had to bend to the wind, right? She'd read that somewhere in her studies of Earth, silently adding to her Earth to-do list, find a mighty oak and see if it bends in the wind.

"I'll follow the rules as best as I can," she promised.

"Another thing, you'll have to stay away from the Big Bang Truck Stop as much as possible and especially avoid my brother Axel and probably my other brother, Diesel. Or you'll have to convincingly pretend you're an earthling."

Her eyes narrowed. "Why?"

"Axel is acting in my stead as security chief while I'm gone the next few days. He's seen the picture your mother gave us. However, he thinks you returned to the ship with your lady's maid and left Earth. He might recognize you even with the bold blue streaks in your hair and wonder why you're here and who is on the ship if you aren't. I'm hoping to avoid anyone ever knowing.

"And if Diesel finds out that I'm seeing an earthling—" let alone harboring an Alpha from an unsanctioned way station ship visit "—he might find a way to shoot you with a Defender."

"Why would he? Besides, it won't work on me, will it?"

"No. But if he thinks you're an earthling, you'd have to collapse and pretend to forget stuff. But if it's known that I'm hanging out with an earthling—because what else could you be—he'd shoot you with reprisal in mind. If you *didn't* fall down and forget like a human, he might put you in the brig himself." *Or shackle you and learn the real truth. Bad idea.*

"Reprisal? Like revenge? I can't wait to hear the explanation for this."

Cam sighed. "I may have shot his part-human girlfriend with a Defender one time. Maybe two times."

"One or two, huh?"

"Okay. Possibly more than twice. It's hard to remember. But my brothers think they are funny and I just want you to be prepared to avoid them to make things easier on us both until the ship returns."

She frowned, not wanting to think about the ship's return, but nodded. "I'll do my best."

"Great. Now that that's settled, where would you like to go first?"

She straightened as the biggest grin she'd ever sported shaped her lips. "Oh, I don't know, but I do have a list of possibilities."

"A list?" He grinned back at her. "Of course you do. Tell me a few items on your list."

"Okay. I want to hike through a forest and see the tallest trees, and also a mighty oak tree, bending in the wind if possible.

"I want to see a really big lake. I want to paddle in a boat across that lake. I want to go to a zoo and see all the earthly animals…and ride a motorcycle… Oh, and visit a biker bar to play pool… And I must make time to go to a big shopping mall to walk around, get my nails done. And if I do nothing else, I must eat in a food court before I go back home."

"A food court? A Biker bar? I'm not sure which of those is more disturbing."

She ignored his comment to ask for clarification. "So is the food court like eating with royalty or like watching lawyers at a trial work while you eat?"

"Um, neither. Not even close. You might be disappointed to discover it is basically crowded, cheap fast-food eaten in uncomfortable chairs that are just as cheap between shopping forays into stores. There aren't many healthy choices at a food court."

She laughed riotously. "You think I came all the way to Earth to find *healthy* choices?" And then giggled some more.

That sexy half-smile shaped his lips. "Touché."

"What does that mean?"

"It's French. It means, I take your point."

"Ahhhh. Okay. Where can we go and what can we do first?"

He hooked a thumb over his shoulder, pointing to his garage. "Well, I do own a motorcycle."

"You do? Really?" He nodded with the kind of look of pride that only the males of their species could pull off without looking foolish.

"Are you in a motorcycle gang?"

"Of course. We call ourselves Hell's Aliens," he said without missing a beat.

"Oh, you do not."

"Maybe I exaggerate."

"Regardless of your fake affiliation to a made-up motorcycle gang, that's what I want to do first. Ride a motorcycle."

"Okay. That, I can do."

"Will you teach me to drive it?"

A mock-horrified look crossed his features before he relented. "If we have time, maybe."

Ria was so excited she put her cup down and moved closer to hug him. Before she could close the distance between them, he straightened and put his hands out. "Wait."

She carefully wrapped her arms around his

neck. "I know what you're going to say and I understand how you feel. Maybe I even applaud it, but I want one last kiss before we cut off all gestures of affection. And please make it good. It has to last me for ten whole days." *Or possibly forever.*

"Touché," he said again and kissed her exactly like it would be their last time.

Cam revved the motorcycle's engine a couple of times, enjoying the way it made Ria tighten her already firm grip around his waist, and headed north on the outskirts of Alienn to avoid any nosy townspeople who might spread rumors or speculate about who he was hanging out with. Especially Aunt Dixie.

Anytime he cruised through Alienn, he encountered no less than three people he knew who wanted to stop and chat. He wanted to be alone with Ria, so he avoided downtown.

The county road around the western side of Alienn heading north to the mining operation was typically not used much for day-to-day traffic. So it was with some surprise that he rounded a long curve in the road to see two sheriff's vehicles stopped about a mile or so ahead, facing opposite directions as the officers had a chat.

He had plenty of time to stop. Luckily, he hadn't

been going as fast as he usually would have, so Ria could look at the scenery, but his heart sank when he realized he knew both of the men chatting it up.

Now he'd be compelled to speak to them and introduce Ria. Then he'd have to hope they wouldn't talk about her to anyone in his family, which was highly unlikely. She'd be the first topic they'd bring up anytime they saw him for the next several years. *'Member that mystery girl riding behind you five years ago? Whatever happened to her?*

The driver's-side windows were both down. The two cruisers were parked about four feet apart, giving Cam plenty enough space to ride between, which he did. He wanted to get the dreaded conversation over with a soon as possible.

On the right side headed in the same direction was Sheriff Hunter Valero, the sheriff of Old Coot, home of the Smokin' Hog Saloon. He was human, but well-regarded in Alienn by everyone who knew him.

On the left was Wyatt Campbell, sheriff of nearby Skeeter Bite. He was also well-regarded by the folks in Alienn and was often mistaken for an Alpha when he visited the Big Bang Truck Stop because of his large stature.

Cam cut the loud engine before rolling the bike between the two vehicles. He pulled his helmet off, tucked it under one arm and nodded once at each of the men. They nodded back.

"What are you two doing out here? Hiding from

the public?" Cam asked, making conversation, hoping he could keep it quick.

"Nope. Just shootin' the bull, is all," Wyatt said, his gaze going over Cam's shoulder to Ria. "So, who's that ridin' with you, Cam?"

Cam pointed his thumb over one shoulder and said, "This is Ria. We're just taking the bike out for a scenic ride." Ria waved, but didn't remove her helmet, for which he was very grateful.

Wyatt and Hunter looked at each other with knowing grins and then back at him. "Ria? Is she from Alienn?"

"No," Cam said quickly. "She's from out of town."

"Is that so? Did you meet her at the Smokin' Hog Saloon last night by any chance?"

"How do you know that?" Cam had always felt rather inconspicuous during karaoke night. Now he knew he'd been wrong.

"Come on, Cam. How do we know anything? There is a wide and active grapevine weaving tales all through the local towns. I know you're aware of it."

Cam ignored what he may or may not know about the local grapevine, asking, "Who was gossiping?"

Wyatt lifted one shoulder and smirked. "I also heard tell that some pretty lady sang a karaoke song directly at you. Two songs, in fact, and that you were obviously smitten the entire time."

Hunter added, "There are also rampant rumors that you promptly took three months off work at the truck stop to go elope, build a cabin on some land, settle down and have a dozen babies."

"Oh, yeah? Was it my aunt Dixie or did my mother call in from her travels with that fantastical gossip?" he asked, not hiding his eye roll. He was glad Ria couldn't see his face, since he could feel the heat of an unmanly blush spreading over his cheekbones.

"I don't rightly remember," Wyatt said with a wink and a grin.

Cam didn't want to deny his feelings, or shoot down the elopement theory—especially since that notion had actually crossed his mind—in front of Ria.

"Don't believe all the rumors you hear or you'll end up knee deep in swamp water looking for a bogus bigfoot in the middle of the night that turns out to be a huge, mangy dog that smells really bad. Trust me on this one." Cam referred to an incident recently in Alienn where an angry Alpha-Prime creature—some Alpha's exotic, illegal pet—got loose and had to be subdued. Only a few Alphas knew the *real* story, and it wasn't a mangy dog, huge or otherwise.

The feral, disobedient gaze of that beast right before Cam slapped the shackle sticker on its neck lived in his nightmares. It had been his idea to pass the whole incident off as fake and trot out a filthy, grungy mutt of indeterminate breeding to show the reporters and keep Alienn's secrets.

"Good point," Wyatt said.

Hunter asked, "Are your folks still traveling around the country in that RV?"

Cam smiled, grateful for the change in subject from both the false rumors of his elopement and the recent creature capture. "Oh, yeah. They'll be back in a month or so for Diesel's wedding. That's the only marriage I'm aware of, by the way."

"That's right, I heard about that. So your big brother is getting married, is he? I can't believe you didn't try to stop him."

"I did try. He just didn't listen." They all traded a few more caustic bites of humor over the demise of Diesel's bachelorhood even though Cam figured his brother was really lucky to have found his soul mate. He was surprised Ria wasn't poking him in the ribs for his views on marriage and bachelorhood. Maybe he should soften his attitude.

"Seriously, though, it turned out for the best. Juliana loves him and he's stupid over her, so I'm sure they'll be good for each other and live happily ever after," Cam said.

"High praise," Wyatt said.

"Does this mean you might be next on the bachelor chopping block?" Hunter nodded once at Ria. "Maybe the gossip following you now will be true one day very soon. My favorite, of course, is the one that has you planning a dozen babies. I'd pay good money to see that show."

"Funny." He was about to add the words "big, fat no" to that, but couldn't seem to get the negative phrase past his lips. Instead, he waggled his eyebrows and said, "You just never know."

The sheriffs laughed. Ria squeezed his waist once. It was long past time to go.

He went through the typical ritual of goodbyes—which in the South often took some time—and finally said, "See you all around."

Cam put his helmet back on, started his engine and revved it for effect. He and Ria both waved goodbye and soon they were zipping along a winding country road past the turnoff for the bauxite mine his family managed and racing further north.

He discovered that the faster he drove, the tighter Ria held on to him. He had to slow for the city limits of Skeeter Bite. He knew the sheriff was otherwise occupied, but didn't want to get caught screaming through town at top speed by one of Wyatt's deputies.

Plus, he believed in safety. The rest of their spontaneous ride was just the two of them and the open road.

Cam enjoyed the ride so much, he forgot where he was. The sign on the road directing them to the Road Rash Pub and Pool Hall only two miles ahead woke him up. He pulled to the side of the road to make a U-turn, but Ria squeezed his waist and poked him several times in the side.

He parked his bike on the shoulder, put the kickstand down and shut the motor off.

"I want to go to the Road Rash Pub and Pool Hall," she said the moment he pulled his helmet off.

"Um. No." He wasn't taking her to a biker bar, no matter what was on her list of fun things to do on Earth.

"Why not? Is it sort of a biker bar or anything?"

"Doesn't matter. I'm not taking you there."

"That means yes. And as you're aware, biker bar is at the top of my list."

"I'm aware. I'm just not as familiar with this bar as I am with other places." He'd been there a time or two, but only in an official capacity, never for recreation.

"I'll be good. I swear. Oh! I know. I can be your biker babe."

"Biker babe? Where did you hear that term?"

"The Earther book I read."

"It's not safe."

"What? For me? I'm not afraid." She was beautiful.

"You should be." He was not taking her there.

"Why? I'll be with you and no one would dare mess with you, Cam. I'm totally safe in your company." She squeezed him around the middle and his resolve weakened.

She wanted to cross "biker bar" off her list and if they were going, afternoon was better than after dark when all the rowdies would be in attendance. Perhaps an afternoon visit to this place was a better choice than any of the other biker bars he knew of in the area. Maybe they could make this a speedy excursion. She pulled her helmet off and shook out her long, dark, blue-streaked hair. Gorgeous.

"Okay, here's the plan. We will go in, drink one beer and leave." Cam looked over his shoulder to confirm she understood his edict.

She shook her head. "Two beers and we have to play a game of pool, too."

"You are testing my patience," he said with amusement.

She lifted up off the seat enough so she could kiss his cheek. "One game of pool, okay? Then I'll be able to cross motorcycle ride, biker bar and play a game of pool right off my bucket list. That's called a hat trick, right? Accomplishing three things?"

"Hat trick is three things, yes. However, a bucket list is what you do before you die, Ria. You have plenty of time."

"No. I only have ten days to do everything on my list and then my life will be over." She dropped to the seat behind him, bouncing the bike as she exhaled a deep, forlorn-sounding breath.

She pushed her helmet back in place, tucking her riotous blue-streaked locks behind her and wrapped her arms tightly around his middle as if she didn't want to discuss anything further. Her tone was so pitiful regarding her future that he almost turned to comfort her, but instead pointed his bike toward the biker bar before he changed his mind. This was probably a really bad idea, but he couldn't deny her the joy of a hat trick of items to cross off her list.

Cam understood. He felt much the same way about his future ten days from now. So he started the motor, revved the engine a couple of times just to thrill her and eased out on the highway toward the Road Rash Pub and Pool Hall.

He'd insist on a fast two beers and an even faster game of pool. However, he couldn't lie to himself. He looked forward to spending the time with her.

The exterior of the Road Rash was as disreputable looking as he remembered. There were only a couple of bikes in the dusty lot in front of the ramshackle building when they pulled in. He rolled the bike to a stop near the front door and cut the engine. Ria jumped from the bike and took off her helmet, unconsciously running a hand through her wind-tangled locks while he dismounted. He took his helmet off, and set both of them on the seat. Ria slipped her arm through his and gave it a tug.

"Come on, let's go!"

Her enthusiasm was infectious, despite his misgivings. "All right, all right."

The atmosphere was quiet as they entered, but the few patrons gathered around the small tables looked in their direction as the door closed behind them. Cam went right up to the bar and ordered two bottles of beer, paid for them and carried them to an open pool table. Ria followed, not saying a word, but the look of wonder and awe on her face made him glad they'd come. He handed her a beer, clinked his bottle to hers in a silent toast and sipped the malty goodness. She took a sip, closed her eyes and sighed. "This is good stuff. I like it."

"And a new beer drinker is born." She giggled and it was all he could do not to press a kiss to her smiling lips. Instead, he put down his beer and busied himself racking the billiard balls into a beat-up wooden triangle.

"Do you already know how to play?" he asked.

"Nope. But you'll teach me, right?"

"Sure thing." He selected a cue stick for each of them. "Have you at least seen it played?"

"Yes. I saw a video, but the guy was an expert doing what they called trick shots."

Cam nodded and explained in general terms how to play as he smacked the cue ball into the triangular group of billiards, spreading them all around the table. She watched carefully, hanging on every word he uttered.

Cam, ever alert to potential security threats, noticed a few people watching them. Ria bent over the table's edge, stretching her stick to reach the cue ball. "Is this right?" she called over one shoulder.

He moved closer to bend over the table next to her and adjust her fingers. "Now try it." She hit the cue ball perfectly. It clacked solidly into the six-ball and shot straight into the corner pocket without hitting either side rail.

She straightened and he moved with her. "I did it!" Ria turned to him with an expression he couldn't ignore. "Did you see that?"

"I did," Cam said, tapping her chin with his forefinger. "Good for you."

She stared into his eyes with such an awestruck expression that he was mesmerized. He lowered his mouth to hers and kissed her gently, retreating two seconds later from a deeper entanglement. He'd momentarily forgotten where they were, in public, in a biker bar, no less. And he wasn't supposed to be kissing her anymore anyway.

Her lips flattened and she stared at his mouth for a moment. Was she about to kiss him harder? Maybe. No. She took one step back. "I want to keep playing. It's still my turn, right?"

"Yep. Go ahead." Cam forced a calmer demeanor than what rioted around inside his body right now. She was difficult to resist.

Ria rounded the corner to the other side of the table, lined up her shot, arranged her fingers on the stick like he showed her and popped the two-ball into a side pocket.

"You're a pool shark, aren't you?" he asked, wondering if she'd found some way to practice pool on Alpha-Prime before her arrival on Earth.

"No. I'm not. I wish." Her infectious laugh sparked a warm spot in his chest. This girl was so special. In spite of his earlier concerns, he was glad they'd come inside to fulfill a few things on her wish list.

"Do you even know what pool shark means?"

"Yes, I do, thank you very much. I'm not a pool shark. I've never played before now. So this is strictly beginner's luck." Her expression was euphoric and he'd be lying if he said he wasn't falling for her just a little harder each moment they spent together. More danger to his heart and soul.

"Okay, hotshot. Go again."

She carefully lined up the four-ball, but didn't hit it with enough force. It stopped an inch from the corner pocket she'd attempted.

"Close, but no cigar, hotshot."

"Drat," she said with a good-natured smile. It seemed being close was good enough for her to be totally happy about what she was doing.

Cam walked around the table, bent over in front of her and shot the fourteen-ball into the corner pocket with a crack. Ria cleared her throat. When he looked over his shoulder, he noticed she was staring at his butt. Nice.

He moved to the left and tapped the ten-ball into the side pocket. It was a miracle he made the shot, since all he could think about was her staring at him…and his butt.

Cam moved to the far side of the table across from Ria. Right before he took his shot, she leaned down, showing an expansive amount of cleavage. He barely hit the cue ball with the point of his stick. The white ball meandered sideways at a weird limping crawl, hitting absolutely nothing on the table but green felt.

"You did that on purpose." Cam straightened and was rewarded with an even better view down her shirt.

"Did what?" she asked, not hiding the effort to get her elbows to meet for maximum cleavage display. "Oh. I'm sorry. Am I distracting you?" She giggled again, abandoning her quest to make her already ample cleavage look even bigger, tilted her beer bottle seductively to her luscious lips and finished her beverage in one swallow. He cleared his throat and attempted to clear his mind, but had minimal success. *Push through, buddy.*

"Want another one?" he asked, gesturing with his bottle as he finished the last swig of his beer.

She nodded. "Yes. Please." Cam signaled the bartender for two more bottles of brew even as he wondered how on earth he'd ever be able to let Ria out of his life in only ten more days. Ten centuries wouldn't be enough time to spend laughing with her.

Chapter 8

Ria watched Cam as he wordlessly ordered more beer for them with just a few hand signals. As the bartender got their second round of drinks ready behind the bar, Ria gazed around the unique space, taking everything in. She wanted to live in this moment and remember every single detail for when she had to return home. The most awesome thing in the world was Cam bringing her here to this biker bar with pool tables.

She was playing pool! On Earth! In a biker bar! She wanted to do a dance, but kept herself under control as best as she could. Her eyes widened and the urge to sing struck her when she noticed a jukebox across the room.

Cam followed her gaze and laughed when he saw the machine. "I suppose you want to make a selection."

"I *so* do." She bounced on her toes, trying to subdue her urge to jump up and down for joy like an overexcited child.

"Do you know what song you want to play?"

"Not until I get over there and see the choices."

He fished in his front jeans pocket for some change and handed her some metal coins. "Here are some quarters. Have fun."

She took the money and forced her legs to walk sedately across the room and not skip and dance like she was in a movie musical. She mentally added "movie night" to her list. Perhaps she'd also add "skipping and dancing" to her list and immediately check them off. Her Almanac of All Things Earthling had been the best purchase she'd ever made.

Once in front of the jukebox, she noted that each song selection was twenty-five cents or three choices for fifty cents. That second option was such a bargain, she couldn't resist.

She selected *Our Lips Are Sealed* by the Go-Go's, *One Way or Another* by Blondie and something called *Lovin', Touchin', Squeezin'* by Journey. She's never heard of the song, but chose it because it listed three actions she wanted to do to Cam with every breath she took. Love. Touch. Squeeze. Kiss. Snuggle. Marry. *Stop it. Be cool.*

Ria headed back to their pool table, navigating her way through the randomly placed tables and chairs. She was two tables away from her goal when she moved past a man sitting alone, chair balanced on the back two legs. She only noticed him when he reached out and grabbed her wrist. She spun on him as the opening line of her first selection thumped through the speakers. The front legs of his chair slammed to the floor.

"Hey, beautiful. Do we know each other? You look kinda familiar to me," he said, tightening his grasp on her wrist. "Why don't you sit with me for a spell so we can get acquainted again? I'll even buy you a drink."

"No, thank you. I already have a date and a drink." She tried to pull her wrist from his grasp, but he held fast.

She tugged away again, harder, but he didn't let go. "Come on, now. You can sit here with me for a minute. Your date won't mind."

She jerked away, but failed to gain her release. Her wrist was starting to hurt. "Let go of me or else—"

"Or else what?" He gripped her tighter.

She paused for a beat, but finished her thought. "Or else my date will beat the snot out of you and I'll cheer him on when he wipes the floor with your limp body."

"That's not very nice," he said with a sneer. She smelled his noxious booze breath and yanked her hand again. He wouldn't let go. A ripple of fear coursed down her spine when she couldn't get free.

"Grabbing my wrist and refusing to let go is not very nice, either."

"Well, I call that dogged determination." He grinned as if it was perfectly normal behavior to grab a girl and refuse to let go. His level of drunkenness must be greater than she thought.

She turned, launching away from him in hopes her wrist would come along with her, just in time to bounce her upper torso off Cam's chest. His arms encircled her body and her panic bled away like water through a sieve. She hadn't even heard him come over.

"Let go of her," he said in a cold, authoritative voice.

"Or else what?" The guy had a death grip on her wrist. He stood up, wobbled a bit, but kept hold of her.

"Or else I'll kick your sorry drunken butt into the next county and—"

A voice from behind them cut off Cam's looming threat. "Randy, let her go or I'm calling the sheriff." The bartender carried their second round of beers on a small tray as he voiced his warning.

Randy released her on the first syllable of his name. "Go ahead, call the sheriff. I didn't do nuthin' to her," he said, leaning back in his chair to balance on the rear two legs again. Ria rubbed her wrist and contemplated pushing the front edge of his unbalanced chair sharply with her toe. Would he get up and fight?

Watching a bar brawl wasn't on her bucket list, but she could add it. She was mad enough to take him down in a fistfight all by herself.

"You grabbed my wrist and wouldn't let go. You call that nothing?" Ria asked, incredulous.

He shrugged. His expression was unapologetic, as if grabbing was part of the whole biker bar experience. Perhaps it was. He stared at her hard again, his eyes traveling from her head to her knees and back up. Ria felt Cam tense as if preparing for battle. She should stop and take this situation down a notch.

The drunken man's gaze ran up and down her body again, stopping at her head. "As a matter of fact, you *do* look really familiar, sweet thing." He pointed to her head. "It's those blue streaks in your hair. We *have* met before, haven't we?"

"No. You haven't ever met her before," Cam said with a glare. He took a step backward, pulling Ria along. "Come on, let's go."

The guy's eyes narrowed and he snapped his fingers. "Wait a minute. I remember now. I saw you singing karaoke last night at the Smokin' Hog Saloon." He glanced at Cam. "And you went home with him, didn't you?" He suddenly sounded aghast, accusatory and critical at the very idea of her association with Cam.

Ria sucked in a loud breath of indignation. "That's none of your business—"

The bartender moved a step closer. "That's it. Go home, Randy. Or I'll call someone you *are* afraid of."

"Oh, yeah? Like who?"

"Like your old lady."

"She ain't my wife. I can do whatever I want."

"Oh, okay. So I should go ahead and call her and tell her what you're up to right now?" the bartender threatened, pulling a cellular phone from the pocket of his jeans.

Randy slammed his chair forward and grabbed for the phone, missing it when the bartender moved quickly. "Now wait just a dang minute. That's not what I said."

Cam pulled his wallet out and offered the bartender some money. "For the second round," he said. "We've got to go."

The man waved away the cash. "No worries. On the house for your troubles."

"Do we really have to leave?" Ria asked. Dang Randy and his grabby drunken antics, ruining her first pool game that they hadn't even finished yet. Plus, they hadn't even listened to all the songs she'd selected from the jukebox.

The bartender said, "Go ahead and finish your game. Randy was just leaving. I'll make sure he don't bother you two again." The bartender smiled, revealing a row of slightly crooked front teeth.

"Okay. Thanks." Cam grabbed the two beers off the tray one handed and walked with his arm around Ria to the far side of the pool table. Randy got up, stumbling and grumbling all the way out the front door.

The bartender picked up his small tray and followed Randy outside. Cam offered Ria one of the beers that had been on the house. She knew that meant free.

"We can really stay?"

"Sure. I guess so. To finish our pool game at least."

"And listen to the jukebox." The second song came on and Blondie belted out the next tune Ria had selected. Cam nodded and a sudden grin shaped his features. "And listen to jukebox music."

He gestured for her to take her turn. She bent down to the task as the front door opened. She expected the bartender to return, but instead saw a tall figure out of the corner of her eye.

"Are you kidding me?" Cam said under his breath.

"What? Who is it?"

"Diesel," he said glumly.

Diesel, your brother, the one I'm supposed to hide from? Ria turned her head toward the front door in time to see the large figure of Diesel Grey in the doorway.

Ria remembered him. Diesel had welcomed the cruise liner's passengers into the way station the afternoon they'd arrived at the Big Bang Truck Stop. Delighted to see someone she knew, sort of, Ria forgot Cam's instructions to avoid his brother and waved.

"I remember him," she said, and continued waving at the man they called the Fearless Leader.

Cam grabbed her hand and pushed it down to her side. "He can already see us, Cam, whether I wave or not." She shot her other hand up and waved again, earning a rather disgruntled look from the man at her side.

"We are trying to be incognito. You only know him because of the way station in the basement. Listen to me, Ria. Do *not* tell him who you are."

"I know. I won't tell him. I can be cool. I'm a cool biker babe." Cam looked at her sideways. There was on odd expression carved in Diesel's features. "On the bright side, it doesn't look like he expected to be seen here either," she said.

"It *is* an out-of-town biker bar," he said under his breath.

"I know," she said, exuberance radiating from both words. She was so happy. Was it the beer? "And it's awesome."

Cam watched their unwanted companion approach with a loud sigh. "I wish you weren't so gleeful about it. Don't forget, you must pretend you are human. And you absolutely do not know him, right?"

"I know, Cam." She was fairly jumping up and down with excitement. The beer had definitely given her a warm, happy feeling inside.

"I knew I shouldn't have brought you here."

A giggle escaped. "Oh, don't be such an old

fuddy-duddy, Cam. It will be fine." She pressed a kiss to his cheek. "And also, in case I forget to tell you later on, I want you to know that this has been the best day of my life."

"Even better than last night?" he said with an amused grin and a wink.

Her face went totally hot with the memory of all the lack of sleep they'd gotten the night before. "You're absolutely right. It's the *second-best* day of my life."

"Cam?" The Fearless Leader stopped in front of them. "What are you doing here?"

"Oh no. You first," Cam said. "I didn't know you were fond of biker bars."

"I'm meeting someone here." Diesel quickly scanned the room, then turned his gaze back to them.

Cam smiled. "Juliana?"

"No. Wyatt."

Does he mean Sheriff Wyatt Campbell?

"You're meeting Wyatt? Why?"

"I don't know yet. He was the one who called the meeting and set the location."

"Why didn't you invite me?"

"Because you took the next several days off for your first vacation in…forever," he said with what sounded like a hint of exasperation. He took a long look at Ria, staring at her hair for an extra beat. She slapped a big grin in place. Did she look human? Did the blue streaks work as part of her Earther disguise? *Why am I grinning so hard?* "But now I can see why."

"Thanks," Ria said brightly. Diesel nodded then put his focus back on Cam.

"Do you want me to sit in on the meeting with you?" Cam's serious security hat seemed to slide into place without warning. She was impressed, but then she wondered what she'd do while Cam left her to own devices to take care of business.

She would be the first to admit she was easily distracted by all the fun and interesting delights Earth had to offer. She would start out trying to be good, but what if another man grabbed her? What if someone else recognized her from the karaoke bar? She needed Cam and he needed her to stay by his side.

Thankfully, his brother turned down his offer. "Nope. You're on an extended vacation now, remember?" Diesel glanced at Ria and grinned. "So for once, enjoy your time off. I'll brief you when you return, if it's anything vitally important."

To Ria, he said, "Hi there, I'm Diesel." She would have known him even if he hadn't greeted the cruise liner's passengers in person. He was sort of famous on Alpha-Prime even for those who'd never studied Earth like she had. Almost everyone knew Diesel Grey was the newest Fearless Leader of the Earth colony.

Cam Grey was listed as the chief of security, but there was no picture of him. If there was, she might have realized who he was at the karaoke bar right away instead of believing he was an earthling named Cam.

The two blackberry martinis she had downed to give herself the courage to get up on stage and sing had obviously clouded her judgment. Side by side, the family resemblance between Diesel and Cam was unmistakable. Would she have made the connection if she was sober?

Maybe. Maybe not. Knowing Cam was an Alpha wouldn't have made her less attracted to him. She noticed him the moment he entered the bar. If she'd known he was an Alpha up front, she couldn't say it would have changed a single thing.

"Hi, I'm Ria. Pleased to meet you, Diesel."

"Likewise. Apparently my brother wants to hog you all to himself, so he hasn't bothered to introduce us. Which is fine. I get it. I even find it difficult to blame him, but the thing is, I already have a soon-to-be wife at home. And I'm madly in love with her, which he well knows, so he shouldn't be so difficult."

"I'm not being difficult," Cam said. "I was *about* to introduce you."

"Sure you were." Diesel winked at Ria, making her laugh.

Behind them, the front door opened and another tall, familiar man dressed in a uniform entered the bar. He lifted a hand in greeting to the three of them as he approached.

Wyatt whistled. "Wow. This is the girl you were hiding behind a helmet on your bike earlier? I can see why."

Cam rolled his eyes. "Ria, you remember Sheriff Wyatt Campbell from earlier."

They shook hands. The sheriff was a pretty big guy, like an Alpha, but she could read his mind. He was definitely an earthling. Wyatt thought she was pretty and he liked the exotic blue streaks in her hair, wondered if it was really her hair or fake hair that she fastened into her locks. But the sheriff didn't have a romantic interest in her. He had another girl on his mind.

Ria thought it was sweet that he was here to talk to Diesel about the girl he thought about...a lot.

"Great to meet you," Wyatt said, his thoughts refocused on the color of her hair...and how the style might look on the girl he loved.

"Thanks. Nice to meet you, too." She pointed to her hair and said, "The blue color is really my hair, not fake stuff fastened in."

Wyatt sucked in a sharp breath. "How did you know that's what I was thinking?"

Drat. She shouldn't have answered his mental questions.

Chapter 9

Cam would hate to shoot Wyatt with his Defender, but might not have a choice. He put a hand on his belt where his Defender typically was, but it was gone. Heaving a mental sigh that his best tool to keep earthlings from discovering aliens was back at home, Cam relaxed and dropped his hand to one side. He'd taken off his Defender along with his regular duties in lieu of spending the day out and about with Ria.

Diesel had a small version on his hip, so that might be an option. Cam glanced around at the seated patrons. Seven other earthlings would be impacted if he yanked Diesel's Defender from him and fired it off in the room. That would leave him with Diesel and Ria staring at each other. Bad idea. That would create even more questions he didn't want to answer.

Better to defuse the situation rather than create chaos in this small bar.

"Everyone asks about her hair," he said quickly.

"She just throws that out to everyone she meets when they stare at her head."

Wyatt relaxed and nodded as if it was a perfectly logical explanation for how she'd just basically read his mind. It seemed to come naturally to her.

Diesel and Wyatt excused themselves to a table in the corner well away from the pool table. Cam should have tried to read Wyatt's mind. He didn't often make the effort, not wanting to know things he shouldn't.

Cam and Ria finished their game of pool and listened to music as Wyatt and Diesel talked, heads bent in serious discussion for a few minutes. Cam gave up on trying to read their lips. He didn't have the skill for it. They were either talking about Valkyries or possibly Velveeta and that's where Cam gave up on his nonexistent skills of lip-reading. The two men finished their conversation fairly quickly and left the bar with a waved farewell to Cam and Ria, not giving him a chance to read Wyatt's mind for information on the meeting.

Whatever it was put an interesting expression on Diesel's face. It must not be about Alienn or anything to do with the secrets they were hiding or Diesel would have given Cam a signal. Wouldn't he? Maybe. Maybe not. Diesel wasn't always as forthcoming as Cam wanted him to be, but maybe only in regard to dating Juliana.

Cam made a mental note to ask what this

conversation had been about when he returned from his vacation. He glanced at Ria. She beamed with joy and that was enough to distract him from any further thoughts about whatever Diesel and Wyatt had talked about. He put his focus where it belonged, on the dwindling time he had to spend with an incredible woman he wished could be his. He watched her line up her next shot.

She was so beautiful, so fun to hang out with…and so going back to Alpha-Prime to marry someone else.

Was she so intriguing because deep down he knew she was unavailable? That question rolled around in his head for several moments before he drew an interesting conclusion. No, her unavailability was not the reason he thought she was fascinating. Cam would be captivated by Ria regardless of any possible future for them. And maybe that was where he should direct his attention, on finding a way to keep her.

Ria came close to beating him in their next round of pool. By then, a rougher crowd started arriving, a few at a time. The newcomers stared possessively at Cam and Ria's pool table like dogs eyeing a rival's chew toy. Cam made the last two shots and won their final game. He relinquished the table with a nod to a biker dressed in black. The dude was completely bald, but had a bushy gray beard that hung nearly to his elaborately detailed motorcycle-shaped belt buckle.

Ria had also taken note of the bearded man, but seemed more interested in taking in his authentic biker look than being intimidated. Perhaps it was something else she could cross off her list. Get a good look at a real biker.

Mostly Cam was grateful she didn't read the guy's mind and blurt out what he was thinking.

As they went outside, Ria looked wistfully over one shoulder. They walked a few steps to his motorcycle. He smiled at the glee evident in her eyes. She reached out and hugged him tight. He wrapped his arms around her and buried his face in her hair.

"Thank you so much, Cam. That was so amazing and so much fun and I'll never ever forget it. Not in my whole life."

"Me either," Cam said. He meant it. He'd never been a biker bar kind of guy, but the experience had been incredible and he knew he'd remember it on his deathbed, even with the annoyance of the drunken dude hitting on her. He liked coming to her rescue.

Cam had studied her at the jukebox, making her selections, but pretended to eye the lay of the balls on the pool table when she turned to rejoin him. When he next looked up, it was to see her attempting to get free of the drunken guy's grasp. He instantly wanted to leap over tables and chairs to get to her.

Luckily, he had sense enough not to make a

bigger deal out of it than what happened. But he'd been ready to. In that first incendiary moment, he would have fought off a hundred bikers to ensure she was safe.

Ria leaned back and looked up into his eyes. They stared at each other as unspoken desire filled the small space between them. The silent fog of craving that he harbored for her, and only her, clouded his thoughts with ideas of what he'd be willing to do to ensure they remained together. Run far away, hiding from off-planet Alpha authorities like criminals for the rest of their lives? No, not a good idea.

Her expression said she wanted to kiss him. Cam stared at the spark in her fascinated yet mischievous gaze, unsure of whether he should encourage her or back away.

It was a foolish waste of time not to step closer, because he'd never discourage her. He'd never back away. Their time was limited. In that moment he vowed to make all the seconds they had together count. She moved closer and so did he.

Their lips were a whisper away from the kiss he knew they both wanted.

Ria knew she shouldn't kiss Cam. But she also knew she might perish if she didn't at least *try* to get a kiss. Just one little kiss wouldn't hurt anything, would it? She brushed her lips on his cheek, very close to his mouth. He didn't flinch. He didn't look angry. He also didn't retreat from her affection.

He turned his head slightly toward her and stared deeply into her eyes with an unreadable expression. Did he want to kiss her or push her away or put her on a transport to a distant planet? All of the above. None of the above. Unclear.

The unreadable expression morphed into a very clear one of desire. He stared at her like a starving man in front of a feast he wasn't allowed to eat, like he might expire if they didn't take the opportunity to kiss.

How to get him to break his previous edict of no kissing?

"Please kiss me," she whispered. "Just one little kiss, Cam." His eyes closed halfway, and a small groan escaped his lips right before he planted his mouth on hers in a lip lock that fairly scorched Ria in her tracks. They kissed and kissed and kissed like they might never stop. Ria was light-headed after only a few seconds, wanting more, wanting the kiss to last forever.

The roar of more motorcycles approaching the biker bar didn't stop them, but the hoots and hollers of several more biker dudes on their way into the bar did. Cam slowly broke the kiss, but his look remained hungry, like he hadn't quite satisfied himself.

He watched the new arrivals walking past them,

nodding at a couple of biker guys entering the bar.

"We should go," he said, not looking at her after rocking her world with that kiss. He picked up their helmets, handed hers over and mounted the bike.

"Okay." Ria climbed on behind him, put her helmet in place, squeezed her arms around his middle and pressed her front against his back. She wanted to stay with him, forever.

If only Dirt Bag FitzOsbern wasn't on his way back from a routine luxury vacation to make her completely miserable for the rest of her life.

Ria clung to him as they rode away from the Road Rash Pub and Pool Hall.

She thought he might take her back to his house, but instead they left Skeeter Bite on a different road than they'd come into it. After only a few miles, she spotted a sign for a town called Old Coot, Arkansas, Population 4,527, according to the sign on the outskirts of town.

After blazing along at a fairly good speed on all the backroads, Cam slowed considerably when he entered the town limits of Old Coot.

He took her to an ice cream shop where they shared something called a banana split. The dessert was cold, sweet, creamy and scrumptious. The most delicious thing she'd ever eaten.

Next, they went to a place called a Natural History Museum. It was getting late and close to closing time, but they had time to see all manner of interesting things, from dioramas of ancient times from this part of Earth to pottery and old clothing, tools, models of Earth animals and birds—there was a plethora of interesting things to see. The best part was holding hands as they strolled through the museum, stopping to look at the displays.

She felt she walked in a happy daze as they returned to the bike, mounted up and put on their helmets. On the way out of town, they passed a sign that said, "Saying Good-Bye to Old Coot? Come again!"

And then she saw a sign that advertised a traveling carnival. In no time, they approached a field filled with tents and strings of lights and intriguing attractions she could see from the road. She started to poke him in the ribs to get his attention, but he was already guiding the bike onto the dirt road leading to a place that proclaimed, "Carnival Tickets Sold Here!"

Cam parked his bike. Pulling his helmet off, he looked back and grinned. "You were about to poke me so we could stop here, weren't you?"

Ria took her helmet off and laughed. "How'd you know?"

"Guess I'm getting better at reading your mind."

"That's probably dangerous."

"Maybe, but I'll take my chances." He gifted her with a bone-melting half-smile that warmed her from her tippy toes to the top of her head.

Ria slid off the back of his motorcycle and

turned to survey the noises and interesting scents wafting by from this carnival place.

"Ever been to a carnival before?" He got off the bike and secured their helmets.

"Nope. But I can't wait to go." She pointed to a large round metal circle. Pretty lights twinkled from the angled beams as dusk fell. "Is that a Ferris wheel?"

"Yep."

"I want to go on that, but it sure goes high in the air."

"Don't worry. I'll hold on to you."

"What if we fall out?"

"I won't let you fall."

She took a deep breath and let it out. "Do you promise?"

"I do."

She put a hand on his arm. "Will you kiss me when we get to the very highest top?"

"Perhaps."

Ria wanted to skip as they strolled over dirt and uneven patches of dead grass that made paths through the carnival. Games of chance and loud bells came from seemingly every direction.

The very first thing they did was ride the Ferris wheel. As their car reached the very top, the wheel stopped. Ria clung to Cam, her heart pounding at the height, but he kissed her and the rest of the world fell away. Too soon, the wheel spun back into motion and returned them to the ground.

Cam bought her a small cardboard box filled with a fluffy, light, buttery, salty treat called popcorn. It was delicious.

One open-tented area held games of chance. She tossed rings. She squirted a water gun. But her favorite game was something called Skee-Ball. At first, she thought it was miniature bowling. She'd read about bowling, but this was different. And apparently she had a knack for the game. Every time she rolled the ball and it hit the very center target, a bunch of little blue connected rectangles shot out of a slot. The more she played, the more blue rectangles she won. In fact, she earned twice as many of them as Cam.

In the spirit of gamesmanship, he gave her his wad of what he called "tickets" so she could trade them all in and acquire a special prize. She was able to get not only a small, black-and-white stuffed animal—a dog with adorable floppy ears—but also two matching black faux leather bracelets with decorative knots, one for each of them. She didn't know what faux meant, maybe plastic, but they now sported matching faux leather bling.

After mastering a new game and collecting her winnings, they walked around looking inside the tents. One was filled with something called quilts. It was amazing. Master artists had assembled little pieces of material and sewn them all together to make beautiful blankets, each completely unique with a variety of creative and colorful designs.

She didn't have enough Earther cash to purchase one as a souvenir, nor a large enough place to hide it from her mother. Not even with a luxury room on the ship. She teared up a bit at the thought of going back to Alpha-Prime, but shook off the sadness.

Ria would enjoy as much as she could while she was here. Tears regarding her future were a waste of time in the here and now.

She'd have a lifetime to cry her eyes out back on Alpha-Prime.

Chapter 10

Cam took Ria back to his place after their long day out and about. He considered the day a smashing success. Ria had added as many things to her list as she crossed off it, but she was elated. Even the carnival had been fun. While he didn't normally enjoy such things, he had a great time seeing Ria enjoy it.

He made a mental list of all the issues he'd need to sort out once his vacation was over. It would take his mind off of missing Ria. Pain blossomed in his chest every time he thought of losing her. Each time it happened, it took longer to fade. He was starting to believe it might only be a matter of time until the pain simply *didn't* fade. *Think of something else.*

Okay. Why was Wyatt meeting with Diesel at a biker bar a good jaunt away from Alienn, and why had they excluded Cam from the confab? Why hadn't Wyatt mentioned his plan to meet Diesel when Cam and Ria met the sheriffs on the highway earlier? Diesel seemed troubled when he left the bar, but it must not be due to an issue with the truck stop or aliens being found on Earth because he didn't even look at Cam on his way out.

Cam shoved that future discussion onto a mental back burner and focused on what was most important right now. Ria. The thought occurred to him during their auspicious kiss in front of the bar and was reinforced by the encore when they were high in the air on the Ferris wheel that his time to savor her sweet lips was limited.

A war raged within him as to whether he was a fool for not spending every moment in Ria's arms, or whether he was trespassing on another man's territory by allowing her to stay with him until the ship returned. He spent about two seconds considering moving Ria to a more neutral place where he didn't have immediate access to her luscious lips, then decided that was beyond foolish.

His main focus should be creating enough memories with Ria to last a lifetime without her. That's where he intended to put his thoughts.

As they walked into the house, Ria said, "Want me to cook something for you?"

"Do you know how to cook?"

"A little bit," she said with that cute smile he'd learned gave away her exaggeration of the truth.

"Oh? What do you know how to cook?"

"I've never done it, but I did watch a video and I'm pretty sure that I could make a sandwich."

He grinned. "No doubt you could, except that I don't have any sandwich stuff."

"Bummer." Her face lit up again. "Oh. I've also seen a video where someone made scrambled chicken eggs in a flat pan."

Cam wasn't a big egg fan and didn't keep them on hand. "Sorry. I don't keep a lot of things to eat here, mostly snacks. If it wasn't for takeout, I'd probably starve to death."

"Takeout?" Her eyes narrowed. "Like fast-food?" She straightened and looked like she was about to add another something interesting to her bucket list.

Before she said anything, he asked the obvious. "Want to go out somewhere to eat?"

"Yes, please!" Ria's expression lit up like a star gone nova. How was he ever going to live without her? He mentally shook off that depressing notion and prepared to head out again.

"Maybe we could try out the food court at the nearest mall." She clapped her hands. *Oh joy.* Then again, seeing her react as though he were taking her on a lavish dinner date was worth eating overcooked mall food any day.

"Whatever you'd like," he said and meant it. He'd do his best to give her that star-gone-nova expression no matter what she asked of him. Her wish was his command. He was sappy, but in a good way. Not like before.

His mood suddenly darkened. Thoughts of the earthling who'd broken his heart into a thousand pieces a mere two years ago hadn't crept into his mind in a long while. He kept the difficult memory away by indulging his foolish whims at the human karaoke bar, hoping to flush the whole waste of his time out of his system.

Cam couldn't help but compare Ria to Shelly, the girl who'd convinced him love would never be a permanent aspect of his life. They were so vastly different, in looks and attitude and almost everything. Well, they had one thing in common—money. The two women came from two different planets in two different galaxies, yet Cam still managed to fall for another female who came from the wealthy class.

Shelly had expensive tastes. She always needed to have the best, do the best, be the best and only ever spent time in the best of the best places. Shelly wouldn't have been caught dead at the mall. And she especially wouldn't have *eaten* at a food court.

In the six months they were together, Cam had burned through every cent he made and then some. The land he'd been in the process of purchasing played second fiddle to any trifle Shelly set her sights on. Cam justified the expense, telling himself he wouldn't need the land when they married because they'd have to leave Earth and live on Alpha-Prime. That was the rule.

Once an earthling discovered aliens lived on Earth, he or she had two choices: face a permanent memory scrub or relocate with their Alpha beloved to a planet a galaxy away.

His recollection of the day he planned to propose to Shelly crept in, further lowering his mood.

He'd thought everything was absolutely perfect until one second before he opened his mouth to pop the proverbial question. The perfect place, the perfect time of day, the beautiful way she looked—as always. He well remembered the nervous, fidgety way he felt as he worked to come up with the perfect words, wanting his proposal to be spontaneous and not sound rehearsed. Perhaps if he'd spent as much time realizing what kind of person she was versus what he wanted her to be, it wouldn't have hurt so much.

Her look of disgust the instant before he would have knelt to ask her to make him the happiest man in the galaxy was seared in his mind, and on his heart.

Cam shook off the bad memory the instant Ria put her hand in his. He lodged a smile in place and headed toward the SUV in the garage.

The nearest mall was not a giant one with several floors and acres of stores, but it was a two-story affair with several escalators. The infamous food court held pride of place in the middle of the mall.

Doraydo, Arkansas, was a college town filled with young people and a ready clientele eager to ring up their charge cards and slap down some dollars at the mall. Cam had grown more familiar with the town since Juliana came into his brother's life. She'd called it home before moving in with Diesel.

Cam kept an eye out for his eldest brother and his sister-in-law-to-be. It would be just his luck to run into them in Doraydo. He hadn't expected to see anyone he knew in the Road Rash, either, until his brother strolled on in. Hopefully Diesel and Juliana had better things to do on a weeknight.

The long drive to Doraydo seemed to take no time at all, thanks to Ria. She was so easy to be with. They talked about their childhoods, him growing up in a house full of siblings and her growing up as the only child. They were still laughing about his antics with his many siblings when he pulled into one of the mall's parking lots.

They held hands easily and naturally, a distinction he didn't miss or try to curtail. She liked holding hands and so did he. As he'd anticipated, her face glowed as she surveyed all the options on offer in the food court. She wanted to try several cuisines, just in case it was her only chance to visit a mall. She started off with a small hamburger and fries from one place, got a taco from another popular fast-food chain stall, mini-corndogs from a third and ended her meal with a giant cinnamon pastry for dessert.

Cam, in an effort to help her try every single offering, ordered sweet and sour chicken from the Chinese place, so she could try a bite—or six—

along with two fortune cookies. He'd never had food court potluck before, but it was certainly fun watching Ria try things he'd basically grown up on.

They demolished most of the food and decided to take dessert back to his place. She couldn't hold another bite, but managed to talk him into an after-dinner java from a bustling coffee shop. They sipped their coffee as they strolled through the mall hand in hand. The nail salon was two stores from the exit. He didn't know how he'd missed it on the way in.

Ria gave him a pleading look that was more eloquent than any words. He could deny her nothing. She fairly bounced into the place, grinning infectiously as the nail specialist showed her different colors of polish.

Perspective was an interesting mechanism. He adored watching Ria experience Earth and what it had to offer an alien from another planet seeing it for the first time.

He would have taken her to the Nebula Nail Salon in Alienn, but Diesel or Axel might spot them there. Not that his brothers ever went to get their nails painted. However, Cam had a healthy respect for the enthusiastic grapevine that wound through Alienn, and it was rooted in the Nebula Nail Salon. If he took Ria there, the gossip mill would churn into action because he didn't typically date—well, he dated, sort of, but not anyone more than once. And never anyone *from* Alienn, either.

The town's nosy Parkers wouldn't let him get away without a wide telephone-tree worthy notice put out to the whole town about his business. They certainly wouldn't hesitate to chat about a beautiful, exciting, and carefree Alpha illegally visiting Earth. Everyone in town knew about Cam's permanent bachelor status. If he so much as drove by the salon in Alienn, all of his siblings would likely find a reason to come out to the center of town and spy on him.

So Cam sat in a chair in a nail salon far from Alienn and watched Ria experience her first earthling-style pedicure. The manicure would come next. The duo was apparently called a mani-pedi. Ria looked euphoric seated in the lounge chair with her feet soaking in the little foamy bath. From what he understood, it wasn't completely different on Alpha-Prime as far as nail beauty regimens went, but the Earth-style experience was supposedly more luxurious because water was used so liberally.

The nail technician clipped, filed and shaped her toenails, massaging all manner of gels, lotions and beauty goops onto her legs before painting her toes bright blue with a sparkly topcoat.

After her toes were painted and her fingernails were done, the technician asked if Ria wanted a free make-up consultation. Ria grinned like they'd just offered her a million-dollar check. It only cost him time, so he nodded and told her he'd wait right outside. He needed a break from all the interesting and pungent smells.

Cam seated himself on a wooden bench directly across from the salon. He had a perfect view of her having what she'd whispered under her breath was *earthling-style* makeup applied.

He also did a little bit of people watching. He figured it came with the territory of being a security specialist. Some part of him was always aware of his surroundings.

It was evening and the volume of shoppers had thinned considerably—a relief, given he half expected to see a horde of citizens from Alienn ready to jump out and discover his secret. Cam was running scenarios through his head as to what he'd do if he saw someone he knew when Ria walked out of the salon.

"Hi," she said. "What do you think?"

He barely stopped his jaw from dropping. *I think you are stunning.* And it had nothing to do with the earthling-style makeup.

He made a big show of studying her face like he was inspecting it, taking in her lively, mischievous eyes, her devil-may-care grin and her luscious, ruby-colored lips. Amazing. "You look as good with makeup as you do without."

She laughed. "Great answer."

"I do my best and you do look very nice."

"Thanks." Ria sat beside him on the bench, close enough for her side to press warmly against his.

She put her hand on his thigh and said, "The good news is that I want to kiss your lips off, but the bad news is it would ruin my complimentary perfect makeup application, so don't you even dare think about it."

"I'm not gonna lie, a large part of me doesn't care if I smear your makeup all over your lovely face if it means I could get even one little stolen kiss from you."

The corner of her mouth quirked up. "Hey, you were the one who set the rules."

He moved dangerously close, inhaling her luscious scent deep into his lungs. "Tell me, do you always follow every rule?"

Ria's eyes widened and her breath hitched. "You know I don't." Her gaze sharpened. "But if you kiss me, this lipstick will end up all over you, too."

"Don't care." He moved even closer. "It's not like I have to explain myself to anyone else." They were as close as they possibly could be without touching. The tiniest gust of air would push them into each other and, more importantly, their lips would connect.

Her gaze swept from his face to over his shoulder. She broke into a big smile and waved at someone. What the—?

Cam turned halfway around to glance over his shoulder. "Who are you waving at?"

But he saw who it was. *Crap*. "Are you kidding me?" he asked the air around him for a second time today, wondering why the universe seemed to be against him.

"He's from Alienn, right? What's his name again?"

Cam pushed out a long-suffering sigh. "Axel."

Chapter 11

"Axel is another one of your brothers, right?" Ria asked, and waved at the man again. "He definitely looks like you."

She'd only caught sight of him because of the way he abruptly stopped walking and stared in their direction. A huge smile spread across his lips and he waved. She imagined he'd recognized Cam. What could she do but wave back?

"He doesn't look that much like me."

She scoffed. "You two could be twins."

"I already *have* a twin brother, I don't need a triplet."

You have a twin brother? That fact took her off guard. Were Cam and his twin identical? Would she be able to tell them apart if she saw them side by side? Could she add that to her list? Try to tell identical twins apart. Also, don't accidentally kiss the wrong one.

Before she could ask the first of twenty questions about his twin, Cam spun back around to face her. He looked rather ashen. "Okay, pretend to be human," he said in a low, urgent tone, as though they were criminals about to be picked up and taken into custody by a Guardsman with the Royal Magistrate Guard. "Do not mention the ship or that you're an Alpha, or anything pertaining to the basement facility at the truck stop. Got it?"

Ria huffed. "I know."

"Why did you wave at him then?"

"He waved first. I was just being friendly and polite."

"That's not a good enough reason."

"Relax, Cam. All humans wave at each other. I read it in my book. It would have looked weird if I hadn't waved back."

"Not all humans wave at each other. *Promise* me you'll behave."

Ria didn't feel much like behaving. "Maybe I will. Maybe I won't."

"Ria, please. Axel has seen—"

Whatever he'd been about to say, he didn't finish it, because the subject of their first little argument was within hearing distance. It was clear Cam was not very happy to see his brother. In all honesty, she'd forgotten they were supposed to be keeping a low profile and avoid his family. Taking trips to other towns and staying out of Alienn didn't seem to be working for them so far, in her opinion.

"Hey, Bro." Axel nodded at Ria and grinned. "So is this the reason you've been gone from the truck stop all day?"

"No comment."

"That means yes." Axel stuck out a hand in her direction. "Hi. I'm Axel Grey, Cam's older, handsomer brother." She smiled at his joke, took his offered hand and they shook. His eyes narrowed and his grip tightened on her hand. "Say, you look familiar. Have we met before?"

Ria forced herself to remain calm. She laughed. "I get that a lot from folks, actually. I must have an ordinary face."

Cam stood up and moved between them, breaking the handshake. "No. You haven't ever met her. Now go away. We're busy."

"First of all, your face is not ordinary. Second of all," he turned to Cam, "is this the same kind of busy that you suffered from earlier this morning when I woke you up?"

Cam tilted his head back in defeat. "Go away, Axel. I'm warning you."

His brother laughed. "Good luck with that." He turned to Ria. "Hey, I didn't catch your name."

"Ria," she said at the exact same time Cam snapped his head forward and barked, "None of your business."

"Ria," Axel said. "Nice name." He made a face at Cam. He leaned closer to her, whispering loud enough for Cam to hear, "FYI, you should be aware of the fact that he's really grumpy when he doesn't get enough sleep."

Ria covered her smile with her hand when Cam made a disagreeable face.

Axel tilted his head. "Are you sure we haven't met?"

"Nope. I'm certain that we've never met before right now this second."

He made a tsking sound and shrugged. "Well, it's great to meet you, right now this second, Ria."

"Thanks. Great to meet you, too."

"I like the blue streaks in your hair."

She brushed a hand over her locks. "Thanks. It's really fun."

Axel glanced at his brother. "Cam is glaring at me. Believe me, if I could stay and torture him, I would, but I'm on an important errand, so I'll say my farewells."

Cam shoved Axel away and turned his back.

"I'm going to remember that, Cam." Axel pointed his fingers at Cam, shaped them into guns and pretended to shoot off a few rounds into the air.

"Don't care, Axel."

His older brother made a quick stern face, but then laughed as he walked away. "Bye, Ria," he called over his shoulder.

Cam exhaled loudly and his shoulders dropped an inch in obvious relief. "That was close."

"He's nice, your brother."

"He's okay." Cam looked down into her face. "He's right about one thing."

"What's that?"

He held out a hand. When she took it, he pulled her to her feet to face him. "Your face is extraordinary, not average or similar to anyone else."

"Thank you."

"You're welcome." They were standing very close together. Their lips were only a few inches apart. She wanted to kiss him. Hadn't they been about to kiss when Axel showed up?

"I meant to thank you for coming to my rescue earlier at the biker bar," she said, placing her palm on his chest. His hand covered her fingers and squeezed gently.

"I think you already thanked me on the way out of the biker bar, didn't you?"

"Still, I should say it again because I was really scared, but I knew you'd protect me."

"Of course. What else could I do?"

Cam moved closer. Ria met him halfway for an achingly sweet kiss. Their lips barely touched for single sizzling second…

"Cam, I forgot to tell you something."

They broke apart like they'd been set on fire. Axel stood two steps behind Cam, wearing a smirk.

"You've got to be kidding me," Cam said under his breath. "What is it?" he asked louder and in a more curt tone.

His brother smiled at his back. "Did I hear you say something about a biker bar, Ria? Did you go out for a ride on Cam's motorcycle today?"

Cam practically growled. "What does that have to do with anything?"

"It doesn't. I'm just collecting gossip."

"Tell me what you came to say or get lost. I guess you know which choice I'm leaning toward, right?" Cam turned and took a step in Axel's direction.

Axel pushed out a sorrowful sigh and closed his eyes as if about to impart something difficult. "It's Aunt Dixie."

Ria thought this sounded serious, but Cam seemed more resigned than worried when he said, "What about her?"

"She took a trip out of town for the next week and a half or so." Axel's eyebrows went up and down a couple of times, as though trying to convey a coded message.

Cam straightened and his doleful expression disappeared. "Really? Where'd she go?"

Axel shrugged. "Don't know, but she took Miss Penny with her."

Who's Miss Penny?

"Miss Penny? Juliana's old neighbor?" Cam was surprised.

Juliana had basically brought the elderly woman with her to Alienn when she moved in with Diesel. Miss Penny was an interesting character with a few untold stories in her past. She had moved into the Starlight Old Folks' Home, which was also Aunt Dixie's pet project, though she rarely seemed to stay there. More often than not, she could be found traipsing around Alienn with his aunt, getting into trouble.

Axel nodded. "Yeah, we've got bets on whether this is some sort of elderly Thelma and Louise sort of adventure or if they just went down to Tunica to gamble. If you want in the pot, you have to cough up ten bucks."

Cam shook his head. "No, thanks." He declined to gamble on Aunt Dixie's crazy antics, although it wasn't really like her to take sudden trips. Then again, she had wacky ideas. Maybe this was some new fundraising scheme.

If there was a dollar to be made for the old folks' home in town, she'd be the first one in line to make it happen, even if she had to leave town to do it.

Cam had bigger fish to fry, keeping Ria out of trouble for the rest of her stay. He'd essentially traded a wild and crazy aunt for a wild and wonderful temporary girlfriend.

"Okay. I guess that's good news. Aunt Dixie out of town, making trouble far away instead of locally will be a nice break. Thank you, but why do I need to know this?"

"You live the closest to her."

"So what? That doesn't make her my responsibility."

"Oh, yes, it does. She's everyone's responsibility, Cam. To that end, that's why I'm even here in Doraydo at the mall that is the only place on planet Earth that sells the super important, very special fish food she buys."

Axel held out a sack Cam hadn't noticed. "Here. Take this."

"I don't want it." Cam wrinkled his nose and put his hands up like in an old-time movie bank robbery. The alternative was to slap the sack out of Axel's hand.

Axel pushed out a long breath. "If you're taking the next several days off, I'll have to cover for you at the truck stop."

"So?"

"So, you live closest to her place. You can stop by her house and feed her fish while she's gone. It won't take long."

Cam crossed his arms and gave his brother his fiercest look. "First of all, the definition of me 'living closest' can be measured in yards, not miles. All of us are closest to her. Second, what if I don't plan to stay in the area? What if we are going camping at Petit Jean Mountain this week?"

"*Are* you doing that?"

A glance at Ria told him she wasn't opposed to camping, if her wide grin was any indication. It was on *his* to-do list of things he wanted to do with her this coming week. She had her list, he figured it was only right he had his.

Cam nodded. "I can certainly make the arrangements very quickly."

Axel rolled his eyes. "Fine. I'll put a timer feeder in the tank."

"Great. You do that."

Axel grinned. "I'd planned to anyway. I just wanted to see if I could get you to tell me your plans for the week. And you did, so that means I win. Now that I've foiled the intense secrecy of your plans, I'm happier than a butcher's dog."

"Well," Cam said in a sarcastic tone, "you do know how important your happiness is to me, but if you bother me again, I'll make sure you're as happy as the butcher's *hog*."

"That's okay. My work here is done." Axel backed away a few steps and waved. "You two have fun now." He turned and walked away, but Cam stared until he was out of sight.

The moment his brother was out of earshot, Ria leaned close and asked, "Where is this Petit Jean Mountain place and do we really get to go camping? Is there a big lake? Can we get a boat and paddle around on the water?"

Cam winked at her. "We could do all those things there, but I have a better place in mind and it's much closer."

"Where?"

"Not too far from my house. I can take you whenever you want."

"Camping?"

He shrugged. "Let me guess—camping is something else on your bucket list."

"Not yet, but I can certainly add it."

Cam was also happier than a butcher's dog, but for a different reason. He was delighted she knew what camping was and was eager to try it. A similar activity on Alpha-Prime was called traveling.

While Petit Jean Mountain had registered briefly in his mind when he'd been making a list of places to take her this week, he wanted her to see the special property he loved. The one he intended to purchase. The one he wanted to build his home on and raise a family. Perhaps he could erase the unpleasant memory of his last visit there with a woman he thought he'd loved.

Or perhaps he was foolish to contemplate taking Ria, the woman he *did* love, to the treasured place where he wanted to build his life and live forever, if he didn't get to keep her.

Ria had read about camping in her Earther book. She'd also seen a few videos about the basics. She was keen to try it, but didn't want to see any snakes or get eaten alive by bugs. Luckily, they didn't have crust-fish here. The disagreeable little critter thrived in most saltwater sources on Alpha-Prime. She wouldn't mind learning how to fish for something nicer than crust-fish.

"How far away is this mountain camping place?" she asked as he took her hand and they headed for the exit closest to where he'd parked his SUV.

"A couple of hours from here."

"Is that too far to go?"

"No. But I know a spot where there is a dock and a rowboat on a lake with a rustic cabin nearby. Then we wouldn't have to travel so far." They came to a stop on the passenger side of his vehicle. "Does that sound like something you'd be interested in seeing?"

"Yes, please!" They were standing close together again. She desperately wanted to kiss him, but figured he'd hit his capacity of letting her have her way. For now. So she backed up a step to give him some space. And to save her recently applied lipstick.

He looked surprised, but then did the same, putting more distance between them.

"Let's head back to my house. We'll have to get to bed early. We want to get there before it gets too hot."

He used his fob to unlock the SUV and opened the door for her.

"Okay." Ria wondered briefly where she'd be sleeping tonight. He likely wouldn't let her snuggle up to him no matter how many vows she made about not jumping his bones if they shared the same bed. Truthfully, she didn't trust herself. It was better if they slept apart.

She knew he had a couch and she expected to spend the night there, even though she wasn't in the doghouse. Not exactly. Not snuggling with Cam sure felt like a punishment though.

It was raining hard the next morning and the forecast for the rest of the day called for pretty much more of the same, so Cam let Ria sleep. He left a note and drove out to the truck stop to fetch some staples to last them the next couple of days.

They tucked in at his house and spent the day watching movies, playing board games and trying not to fall more in love with each other, even though that seemed a wasted effort from his perspective.

Late that evening, Cam made a fire in his rarely used fireplace to roast marshmallows for s'mores. Ria added the fireside treat to her bucket list and crossed it off, declaring s'mores her favorite treat so far. She liked lighting her marshmallow on fire until it was completely charred before making her warm, gooey chocolate graham cracker sandwich.

They fell asleep on the fake white bearskin rug he put in front of the fireplace and snuggled together, but fully clothed. Pity. However, it did mean he'd succeeded in keeping his vow for one more day. Yay.

Every day they found a different place to go to fulfill the constant demands of her bucket list. Each and every night, it got harder and harder to keep his hands off her. She didn't make it easy on him, either. She wanted to thank him with a kiss after each and every new item she tried and delighted in.

They hadn't slept together since karaoke night, but rebuffing her each night took a heroic effort on his part.

Cam wanted nothing more than to make Ria a permanent fixture in his life.

Chapter 12

Two days until the Royal Caldera Forte returns to Earth

The week since their big day at the biker bar, carnival and mall had flown by for Cam.

A zealous photographer hired by the town to take photos of the crowds thronging the main street for a fair in Old Coot had snapped their picture another day while they'd stopped to look at a woodcarver's wares. Cam had almost had a heart attack, but Ria said not to worry so much and told him not to be an old fuddy-duddy. The pain in his chest returned when their photo ended up on page three of the local paper.

He told himself the picture was so small, no one could recognize them. If they did, the phone calls from Alienn's nosy Parkers would have flooded his line before the papers hit the welcome mats in time for coffee and toast.

Somehow, they'd dodged another bullet and he was grateful.

He and Ria spent every single moment together. They had done lots of different things on their mission to get through her extensive list. She crossed many things off, but added just as many items as she drew a line through. They laughed. They talked endlessly about everything. They barely slept, each and every night staying up into the wee hours talking about anything and everything they could think of. It seemed neither wanted to waste a moment of their dwindling time together.

Cam found himself mulling the increasing problem of how he'd ever live without her. He knew if he let her go without a fight, he would regret it for the rest of his life.

His viable ideas were few. One was to go on the run with her on Earth. That meant never again spending a peaceful moment. The Royal Magistrate Guard Special Elite Trackers were relentless. They'd search for Cam and Ria until they were caught, tried for their crime on Alpha-Prime and sent to live out their days on a gulag.

He put that idea out of his mind and focused on today's destination—the special property a few miles out of town he'd promised to show Ria. It was the very butt crack of dawn, and he was weary after a restless and mostly sleepless night on the futon in his spare bedroom.

When he'd first explained the sleeping arrangements, Ria had looked forlorn at the idea of sleeping alone in his bedroom each and every night. She didn't say a word in disagreement, but he didn't think her silence on the matter would last. Or maybe he just hoped it wouldn't.

He'd half expected her to put her foot down last night and demand they sleep in the same bed, but she seemed to be making an effort to follow his stupid no-sleeping-together rule.

Two more days together would be both an eternity and a mere snap of his fingers.

"So, where are we going?" Ria asked, her sleepy tone completely adorable.

"It's a piece of property owned by a good friend of mine." *Hopefully it will be mine one day very soon.* He turned off the main road and onto the access road leading to the property. "We're almost there. Up here at the gate is the property line. But I have the combination to the gate lock to get in."

"And this *friend* of yours won't mind if we go there today and look around?" Her mood seemed hopeful, like she actually wanted to see his future land.

"Nope. It's a piece of property I'm thinking about buying. And maybe I'll put a house on it someday." *Actually, I'm halfway to ownership and maybe I'll fix up the existing cabin, too.*

"Really?" She seemed awestruck at the idea of owning property and putting a home on it. Perhaps hopeful was a better word.

A warm feeling rose in his chest, one he batted

down immediately. He should keep his guard up. Shelly hadn't been difficult at first, either. She had looked on with interest when he opened the gate to usher them in. It was after that when things went downhill.

Cam looked out at the land on the way to the property he loved as the warm feeling filled his chest once more. He loved this place. He couldn't wait until the property was all his.

"I come out here a lot to dream and scheme," he said offhandedly. He put the SUV into park, unbuckled his seat belt and opened the door before looking in her direction.

"Dreaming and scheming sounds like lots of fun." She turned toward him with such a look of longing it was all he could do to keep from pulling her close and kissing her the way he wanted to. He was used to firming his resolve where Ria was concerned. He had to do it pretty much every time he looked at her since they'd met.

"It *is* fun," he managed to say. "At least *I* think it is." He wanted her to be interested, but was unsure if she was serious or humoring him.

"I'd love to own a piece of land and live on it, especially if it looked like this. It is beautiful here." Her wistful tone sounded sincere.

Cam cleared his throat. "But you probably live in a palace. I can't imagine you'd like living a hard-scrabble life on a piece of property without all the luxuries either of our worlds has to offer."

"There's where you're wrong." She stared across the serene landscape. "I'd do almost anything to get out of the life I'm about to be forced into on Alpha-Prime."

Out of habit, he said, "Anything?" in a super suggestive tone. It was a joke he and his brothers perpetuated. One would say he'd do anything to get out of a certain punishment, for example, such as work an extra shift. Invariably, another brother would say, "Anything?" in the weighted tone and the first brother would yell, "The extra shift! The extra shift!"

Ria's expression filled with a level of anguish he wished he wasn't impacted by. "Almost anything," she said again. She focused her attention out the windshield at the land he loved.

He got out of the SUV and went to the gate, fumbling with the lock.

The two-year-old memory of when he'd almost ruined his life slipped into the forefront of his head before he could stop it. He should remember it well. He should keep it close to his heart as a cautionary tale.

Worse, he couldn't shake the feeling that if he asked Ria to marry him today, right now—as he almost had asked Shelly on this same piece of property—that she would react the same way his old girlfriend had, with utter and complete disdain.

Did he have the courage to face another contemptuous rejection?

The ugly memory of his halted proposal tortured him as he unlocked the gate to the land he adored, wishing he wasn't the only one who wanted to live out here. He pushed the barrier wide, and hoped this wasn't another colossal mistake.

The day he'd brought Shelly to see his land had been much like this one. The sun rose fast in the clear-blue morning sky, birds sang and a slight breeze made the intense humidity manageable. He'd cleaned out the ground-floor master bedroom of the ramshackle cabin to share with her the beauty of waking up to the stupendous view.

He wanted Shelly to love each of the twenty acres of his pride and joy, even though loving and marrying an earthling meant he could never live here as he'd once dreamed. So instead, he spent his money on the expensive engagement ring he knew Shelly would expect.

The ring burned a hole in his pocket both on the way to his land and even worse on the trip back to town, his question unasked. At least he'd gotten some of his money back from the jeweler.

Shelly had slowly and carefully exited his vehicle, looked around at what he considered beauty personified with a frown.

"What do you think?" he asked.

She didn't have to say a word. Her disdain would have filled ten sports stadiums to overflowing.

"I think I'm ready to leave now." A honey bee buzzed around her head and she swatted at it viciously.

"What? Already? I haven't even shown you the cabin." Cam softened his exuberant attitude, hoping she only teased him.

It took a fraction of a second to realize she was serious. Anger filled her gaze when she said, "In no uncertain terms will I ever live out in the wilderness with a bunch of wild animals, slimy reptiles or a million bugs swarming around trying to sting me, not even if you were the richest man on the planet."

Cam kept waiting for a smile that never came. "What are you saying? You're only looking for a rich man?"

Cam was not, nor would he ever be, considered wealthy. Well, he was rich in friendship, rich in family, rich in siblings and rich in his love for living on Earth. If he married Shelly, he'd have to give all that up to move with her to Alpha-Prime. He'd warred long and hard with himself over his decision to give up everything for the woman he loved.

"That's right. But you aren't rich, are you, Cam?" she'd asked with a sneer. "Not even close." She pushed out a weary sigh, as if she hated being forced to have a long-overdue conversation.

"Why are you with me if you're looking for a wealthy guy?" he'd asked, still not fully cognizant of her ultimate declaration.

"Good question."

"What does *that* mean? I thought you loved me. I thought you loved spending time together."

She shrugged. "I've come to realize that *if* we stay together you'll never be able to give me the kind of luxury I desire. Certainly not as a grease monkey at a truck stop in South Arkansas, I imagine. You'd have to do much better than the job you currently hold. But you like working with your insanely large family at that low-rent truck stop, don't you?" The question sounded more like an accusation.

Cam was still stuck on, "If we stay together." That had been the first of several canary-keeling-over-in-the-coal-mine moments regarding their relationship and how blind he'd been to the truth. Her attitude also brought the first inkling of panic and made Cam wish he hadn't brought her to this beautiful place. She wasn't worthy.

Watching Shelly morph from the sweet yet determined young woman he thought he loved into the shrill, unkind, mean-spirited soul he didn't recognize had been a harsh lesson. It only got worse.

"Are you joking?" Cam said. "I love this place. I love my insanely large family. And I especially love my job, which is not grease monkey, by the way. Please tell me you're joking, because your whole spoiled-rotten brat approach is not funny or appreciated."

"No. I'm not joking, Cam. I'm not trying to be

funny." Shelly crossed her arms in a stubborn move he should have seen coming from a mile away. "I want a different kind of life than the one I've been raised in. It wasn't bad, but I want to live better. I want to have more money than I need always at my disposal. You don't even take me out to dinner anymore."

Cam had spent everything he had keeping her entertained. He was broke. If he kept it up, he'd have to take out a bank loan. Yes, he had enjoyed the fancy dinners, but he never thought she wanted to live like that *all* the time.

She hadn't wanted to come out to his property. She hadn't wanted to learn what surprise he had for her. She hadn't given him the chance to ask his important question before she pooh-poohed not only the land, but also his job and, of course, him.

He was a fool to bring another woman he cared about here. Showing her the land was like showing her his soul.

Cam looked at Ria, waiting for him in the SUV. A faint smile parted her lips as she took in the nature around them. She seemed captivated. Well, she would be. This place was nothing like their desert-dry homeworld. As far as he was concerned, it was paradise.

If he'd married Shelly, an earthling, he would have had to give this place up. If he married an Alpha, like Ria, he wouldn't have to give anything up to be with her.

Was he going to try again?

Ria was *not* Shelly. What he'd felt for the earthling was nothing compared to what he felt for his rebellious Alpha with blue-streaked hair.

He tried not to think about the fact that this joyful journey together on Earth would come to an end in a mere two days. How could he live without Ria? What crazy plan was he willing to instigate in order to keep her here with him?

Any plan, crazy or not, that keeps us together.

He wanted to show her what was important to him. He wanted to show her the land he'd spent the better part of two years since his break with Shelly doing his best to save the money to buy.

Today was an important day, a pivotal day in deciding if they had a chance of making it over the long haul. Today he was showing her the land he loved. The land he'd been prepared to give up for someone who ended up not being worthy.

Only one thing cracked Cam's certainty that Ria had nothing in common with Shelly—wealth. Ria had been raised with it and Shelly wanted more of it.

He guessed when it came right down to it, today was a test. Only Ria had no idea.

Cam needed the answer before he could move forward with any plan to try and break up her arranged marriage and keep her with him forever. He had an idea of how to get that answer, but it was not very honorable.

Cam hopped back inside his vehicle. He guided the SUV through the open gate, deciding not to close it behind them. They likely wouldn't be long. Cam was prepared for the worst, but a little beacon of hope remained in his heart.

Not wanting to jinx anything, Cam didn't say anything or look in Ria's direction until he got to his favorite spot. He drove along the narrow dirt road leading over a small hill. At the hill's crest, the view was perfect. The edge of the lake, the wooden dock leading out to the water and the old cabin could be seen all at once. He loved it.

Beside him, Ria sucked in a deep breath. "Ooh, it's so beautiful, Cam."

Her awestruck expression sent a rush of newfound hope to fill the previously cold spot in his heart.

Cam pulled his vehicle up next to the cabin and parked. He hadn't even gotten it into gear before Ria popped open her door, jumped out and raced toward the dock. He quickly got out and followed her to the water's edge and the long row of sturdy wooden planks leading out into the lake.

"Look at all that water. It's so lovely. So perfect. I love it, Cam." She pointed at the cabin. "And I love the tall old wooden house, too."

"It's called a cabin."

"A cabin," she said as if tasting the word on her tongue and finding a new flavor she liked.

"It's a rather ramshackle old place. The outside

is very weathered and so is most of the inside, but it's definitely interesting in there, too."

"I'm sure it's perfect." She twisted back to stare at the lake, dropping to sit on the roughhewn wooden planks of the dock. She crossed her legs and stared from all the way left to all the way right.

Cam lowered himself to sit beside her. He wasn't even fully seated when she hugged him around the middle. "Thank you so much, Cam. Thank you for bringing me to this wonderful, magical place. I truly love it. It's my favorite place so far. We should have come here sooner." She transferred her hug to his neck, leaving her arms around him as she studied the lake. The wind picked up, sending wavelets across the water to lap against the dock posts.

She rested her head on his shoulder and stared out at the water as if transfixed, releasing a long sigh of what sounded like utter and complete happiness.

Cam circled his arms around her and they sat quietly, simply watching the surface of the lake ripple in the early morning sun.

"I love you, Cam," she whispered as another soft sigh escaped her lips.

Chapter 13

Ria said the words she'd longed to shout since waking up in Cam's bed the morning after her karaoke bar adventure. He was perfect in every way and each day they'd been together proved that truth a little more.

Each time the phrase, "I love you, Cam," bubbled up inside her, she'd tamped it down because she was afraid he wouldn't reciprocate. What if he planned to be through with her once she was gone? What if he didn't want to hurt her feelings before she was safely away from Earth and locked in a life she hated on another planet? A tiny, depressing voice inside her head warned he was only counting down the days until she left, being nice only because their time together was limited and if something happened to end her stupid arranged marriage, he would stutter and find some reason to break her heart.

An equally vocal optimistic voice was certain that of course Cam loved her as much as she loved him. They were obviously meant to be together forever and if she could get out of her engagement to Dirt Bag FitzOsbern, he'd drop to a knee and propose earthling-style in an instant. She wanted that so much, it brought tears to her eyes whenever she thought about it, so she shoved it from her mind as much as possible on a daily basis.

At this juncture, Ria simply hoped he cared about her and didn't want her to leave him forever, never to be seen again on Earth.

Once the provocative, "I love you, Cam," hung in the air, Ria became hyper alert to everything Cam did. Good news, he didn't stiffen in her arms so much as startle the moment she uttered the heartfelt but totally inflammatory phrase. It felt more like he was surprised rather than horrified. She hoped. Was that a good sign? Or a bad sign? Or perhaps an indifferent sign? Unclear.

She squeezed him harder, afraid he would say that although he really liked her a lot, he didn't feel the same deep affection she'd expressed. Or worse, somehow dismiss her feelings as foolish or impulsive or silly schoolgirl fodder. He didn't. He also didn't move or utter a single syllable. But she got the sense he was at least carefully considering what she'd said. Perhaps he wanted to ensure he responded the right way. Or perhaps he'd never respond, ignoring her earnest declaration of love no matter how many times she repeated it. Should she repeat it? *No. Shut it.*

They remained silent and still, watching the

beautiful water together. The surface of the lake was mostly smooth, but every so often a leaf or something would fall from one of the many impossibly tall trees and the resulting ripples near the shoreline were mesmerizing. Then the wind came up and gentle waves grew in the center of the small lake, rushing toward shore. Ria could have sat with Cam until the sun set.

After a long silence, he shifted and said, "Want to see inside the cabin?" His voice was hushed, but after so much silence it seemed loud. He didn't sound dismissive or angry, so she decided either he didn't hear her declaration or didn't plan to address it quite yet.

"Yes," she said. "I'd love to see inside the cabin."

He stood up, reached a hand down. She placed her palm against his and he pulled her to her feet. He didn't try to hug her or kiss her before starting toward the tall cabin. She grabbed his hand as they approached the porch steps, slipping her fingers in between his. He squeezed her fingers as they walked.

No matter what he said, she loved him. She would love him until the day she died. She wished above all else that he at least cared and would remember her fondly once she was gone.

He entered a six-digit code—that she memorized without meaning to—into the number pad mounted on the doorframe and opened the rustic door to reveal an equally rustic interior. All wood as far as the eye could see. Dusty surfaces as far as the eye could see, too.

She sneezed twice in rapid succession.

"Bless you," he said. "It's pretty dusty in here, but—"

"I love it."

"You do?"

Ria nodded. She couldn't help the goofy smile that shaped her mouth as she tilted her head to look up at the tall ceiling. Both walls on either side came up at long, straight angles to connect at the apex of the ceiling in a point. An elaborate fixture with many lightbulbs and clear crystal ornaments hung from a metal pole in the center of the ceiling.

"It's like a cathedral I saw a picture of once from another country on this planet."

Cam also looked up. "This cabin is what's called an A-frame design. Like the capital letter A in the alphabet, I guess."

She nodded. "Like two cards of chance leaning against each other. It's very tall."

"Three stories," he said proudly.

He was right to be proud. She could see two staircases from the front door and straight ahead. One went from the ground floor left to right and from the floor they were on to a platform on the next level. The other went from the right on the next level to the left up to the top platform. It was all open to the three-story high room they stood in.

Windows filled the front of the cabin, giving them a wonderful view of the lake.

"What's up there?" she pointed to the upper levels.

"There is a bedroom on the second floor and a bathroom, more or less, since it's pretty old and ugly, plus another bedroom on the third floor loft space."

"And on this level?"

"We're standing in the living room." He gestured to the right and a tall counter with two stools like at a bar, and beyond it to what looked like a kitchen that had seen better days.

Cam said, "The kitchen is old and needs a desperate makeover, but I think it would be possible to remodel it. Down the hallway there is another bedroom, another bathroom, a small pantry and a place for a washer and dryer, but I don't know if one was ever installed."

"Are you going to live here someday?"

"That's my plan. I mean, I'll fix it up and everything."

She nodded, wishing she could stay and help him fix this place up. She could add it to her bucket list, remodel a house and make it a cozy home. Probably she'd need more than two days to make that happen. A sudden and heartbreaking sadness filled her. She wouldn't be the one helping Cam make this place amazing. She would be a galaxy away and miserable.

Commuting from Alpha-Prime would be impossible, of course. A swell of anger rose within her and burst, but she tried her best to tamp it down. It didn't do any good to be angry. Mentally, she inhaled and exhaled the foolish anger out, telling herself to focus on the precious time she had left with Cam and not to waste her energy on the overwhelming feelings of unfairness that took up too much space in her mind.

Cam said, "Once upon a time I'd thought about just bulldozing the whole grimy, filthy place into a pile of kindling and starting fresh—"

"Oh, no. You aren't really going to do that are you? Don't tear it down." Her gaze scanned the dusty surfaces and spider-web-filled corners with horrified dismay as if a demolition crew would blow the place up in front of her eyes.

"Nah. I decided not to re-build. The thing is, I love all the views from this place. My favorite part is the view from the bedrooms. They are all gorgeous."

"I'll bet they are. I'm glad you are fixing it up and not tearing it down. I love this place. I'd live here in a second." *I wish I could stay and help you make it perfect.*

"Would you like to see the rest of it, dusty corners and all?"

"Yes, please. Give me the grand tour." She'd read that phrase in her book. The *grand* tour was probably always the best one anyway. "I'd love to see all of it, the dusty corners, too."

Cam walked down the dark hallway and opened a door on the left. A vast amount of light escaped from the open door. She followed him into a lovely room that had already been cleaned up, dust removed and there wasn't a single spider web in sight. The bed was made up with a charming quilt like what they'd seen at the carnival. The spotless floor-to-ceiling windows facing the lake gave a spectacular view of the dock, the trees and the water. This was heaven.

She sucked in a breath and raced to the window. "Oh my goodness, it's so beautiful, Cam. I'd give anything to wake up to this view every single day."

"Would you?" he said from a distance behind her.

She spun around. He had an odd expression on his face.

"I would," she insisted.

He didn't say anything at first, but seemed unconvinced.

"With me?" The look on his face and the sound of his voice said he didn't expect her to want to live here with him, which was completely crazy.

"Of course with you, Cam. Who else would I live with?" A thrill ran down her spine at the mere idea of running away from her odious arranged marriage to a pampered, spoiled-rotten man she loathed and all the obligations she faced on Alpha-Prime. Leaving it all behind to stay here in what was surely paradise—dusty corners and all—with the man she'd fallen in love with was as perfect as a dream. Because she did love him.

Ria loved Cam with all her heart and soul.

She didn't care they'd only known each other for a week or so. She didn't care if they lived in this dusty cabin forever. She didn't care if they never had two nickels to rub together, like she'd read about in her almanac, as long as they were together.

From the moment she'd spoken to him at the karaoke bar, she'd known he was unique, special and perfect. She'd never wanted anything as much as she wanted to spend the rest of her life with Cam.

Not only because of the time they'd spent together in bed, which had been utterly amazing. She genuinely liked him. She liked talking to him. She liked doing everything with him, from fishing to grocery shopping to playing pool while drinking beer in a biker bar. She liked being his biker babe.

She liked when he protected her from rowdy guys in biker bars. She liked when he stared at her as though she was the only girl on the planet after getting her nails painted. She liked that he chose the honorable path with regard to her coming arranged marriage, although she hoped she could get out of it.

Ria especially liked sitting with him watching a calm lake while they held hands and didn't talk at all. She liked getting up early, sipping coffee and taking little road trips around the area of Alienn with him as he pointed out things in the scenery and the wonderful world of Earth.

The amazing and exciting days she'd spent with Cam made Ria realize she could not marry Dirt Bag FitzOsbern. She just couldn't. But she was trapped.

There were only two ways out. One was abuse. Dirt Bag wouldn't even look at her let alone touch her, romantically or otherwise. He considered her tainted with the formerly-rich-but-now-impoverished disease. Unless he became a wife-beating monster, Ria's only way out of this coming wedding was the second option. Her mother had to break the marriage agreement with the FitzOsberns.

Ria moved closer to Cam. "If I didn't have this arranged marriage hanging over my head, I'd bop you over the head and drag you into my life forever."

One corner of his mouth turned up. "Is that so?"

"It is."

"You wouldn't have to bop me over the head, you know. I'd come willingly."

"Good to know." Ria didn't trust herself not to tackle him to the bed surface and have her wicked way with him. He was trying to be honorable and she was trying to let him.

"So what would it take, do you think? Money?"

"To get me out of this arranged marriage?"

He nodded, staring at her as if he had a few less

than honorable thoughts circling around in his head, too.

"Even if Dirt Bag wanted to call it off—I'm pretty sure he does—my mother has the final say. She is the only one with the power to veto or discard the agreement signed twenty-five years ago. Trust me. She wouldn't do that in a million years."

"I see."

"What are you thinking? Do you have some sort of plan? Maybe it's one I haven't considered."

"What if you get married to someone else before the ship comes back?"

Ria's optimism died. A long, forlorn sigh escaped her lips. She'd thought of that. "My mother would have the option of dissolving any partnership so I could complete the terms of the arranged marriage."

He drilled an intense gaze into her face and opened his mouth, but Ria knew exactly what he was thinking. "Not even if I carried another man's child would the arrangement be called off."

Cam's lips flattened. "That's really too bad."

"Why?"

"Because I love you, too, Ria. I'd love to marry you. I'd love to live here with you. I'd love to have babies with you, as many as you want. And I'd love waking up to this view with you every single day for the rest of our lives."

Chapter 14

Cam waited for her to shoot him down and tell him she'd never marry a truck-stop grease monkey. But she didn't. She smiled so hard, tears came down her cheeks.

She launched herself in his direction. He caught her in his arms as her legs wound around his waist. She stared deeply into his eyes, lowering her lips slowly to his for a sweet kiss, then another kiss, then a deeper kiss, then another, and another. He was losing his capacity to be honorable with each electric connection their lips made.

He sat down on the foot of the bed, hugged her tight and pushed his face into her neck, stopping the glorious kissing, instead picking up the enticing scent of her perfume. She pressed her lips to his forehead then leaned her cheek against his head. They clutched each other close, as if daring the world to bother this perfect moment, rocking back and forth slightly with the sheer force of their love for each other.

Cam didn't know how long they stayed that

way, but soon enough they both realized and came to understand the reality of their situation. The longshot of ever being able to live together happily ever after was as far out of reach as it had been the moment they met.

Ria whispered, "As soon as the ship docks, I'm going straight to my mother to tell her that I can't marry Dirt Bag. I'll do whatever I have to do. Say whatever I have to say to change her mind."

"I'll go with you and help convince her."

Ria pulled away. "No. I'll go alone. I don't want her to see you or say bad things to you. And she would. She can be...well, unkind when something isn't going her way. Even if you were the perfect man, and you are, she'd still put you down, I'm afraid."

"I don't care." Usually the mothers of girls he dated liked him, including Shelly's mom. He was considered a catch in many Arkansas circles, including Alienn. He was gainfully employed. He had all his hair and all his teeth, a truly big bonus in some circles.

"Well, I care. I don't want to subject you to her anger. And trust me, she will be furious about this."

"Because of the money." Cam had already met Ria's mother and she was not impressed with him at all. This he knew for a fact. He'd always be a low-life security man in her eyes, tack on truck-stop grease monkey to that assessment and she might kidnap Ria to a far-flung galaxy to keep her away from him out of pure spite.

"Yes. And the prestige of being connected to a Technician's family even by marriage definitely widens her social reach on Alpha-Prime."

Cam understood exactly what she meant. He was never someone who pursued money or pretended he had more than he did. However, Shelly had wanted that kind of life, and for a while, he'd tried to give it to her. He was grateful it only took him six months to catch up on his finances once she was out of his life for good. There had been lots of overtime and several odd jobs involved to make that happen, but it had been worth it.

"If I had a bunch of money I'd offer it up, but I don't. Maybe you should reconsider staying here with me. I'm never going to be able to give you a palace to live in."

She looked over her shoulder at the spectacular view out the bedroom windows. "I don't want a palace. I want to live here." Her stubborn attitude-filled answer made him want to laugh.

"Spiders and all?" he asked.

She frowned. "I'd prefer the spiders lived outside, but yes, I want to live here. I'm even going to add a new item to my list."

"What's that?"

"Restore a lake view, fixer-upper cabin in the woods, of course."

Cam grinned so hard he thought his face might split open. "I'm happy to hear that."

"Are you?"

He nodded.

"How happy are you?" she asked in a sassy tone. Her gaze fixed on him as she started moving closer. He'd be powerless to stop her if she kissed him or hugged him or pushed him down on the bed.

"I'd have to say I'm very nearly rapturous."

She gave his shoulders a determined shove. Cam fell backward onto the bed with her cradled in his arms. Once the bed springs stopped squealing and the bouncing ended, they stared at each other, locking equally intense gazes like there was nothing else to worry about. Like the horrid deadline they faced in less than two days didn't matter. Like the cold, hard separation timeline looming didn't perpetually threaten to freeze them with a big dose of reality at every turn.

Cam leaned up and kissed her tenderly. She kissed him back with a ferocity he wasn't expecting, but enjoyed nonetheless. He certainly didn't curb her desire in the least, although he likely should.

When Ria eventually broke the kiss, they both panted with the delicious effort. He vowed not to go too far, knowing it was an empty pledge. He wasn't certain his previously proclaimed honor could withstand the raw, emotional and frantic sentiments swelling around them.

His communicator buzzed.

Ria made a face while Cam pulled the noisy device off his belt and answered curtly, "What?"

"It's me," Axel said, sounding abrupt himself. "Don't hang up. I fully understand your current circumstances, but I need you to come to the basement facility immediately. Something has happened."

"What?" he asked a second time, managing to moderate his tone.

"I'll explain when you get here. Bring Ria with you."

"Why?" Cam was careful not to say too much with Ria listening so closely.

"I finally remembered where I've seen her. The blue streaks in her hair don't hide the mischievous look in her eyes, Cam. Alexandria Latham Borne is *not* currently aboard *Royal Caldera Forte*."

"I see. Yes. You're right, of course." Cam's eyes closed. He didn't want to look as panicked as he felt with Ria staring at him. "Who else knows this…information?"

Axel made a huffing noise. "No one. I wouldn't tattle on you, Bro. It's not my style to rat out folks, especially not my brother. At least until I've heard his side of the story. And I'm certain it's a good one. Are you on your way?"

Cam didn't want to give up a single second with Ria. "Actually, I'd planned to come back day after tomorrow. You know, once the ship returns and docks."

"Sorry, Bro." Axel did sound like he hated to say it. "But you need to come in right now. It's an emergency."

"Tell me."

"An Alpha woman was brought below stairs with an acute illness an hour ago. Her presence is unexpected."

"Who is it?"

"She was too sick to speak when she arrived, but her aunt and two cousins who accompanied her said her name is Prudence."

Prudence. Where have I heard that name before?

"Prudence?"

Ria looked at him with a question in her eyes. She clearly recognized the name.

Axel lowered his voice. "You remember, Cam. Prudence, the lady's maid who supposedly fetched Alexandria Latham Borne from wherever she'd escaped to on Earth before the ship departed on its ten-day trip, eight days ago.

"But now I know that both Alexandria and Prudence are still on Earth. So it begs the question, who in the hellish and holy space potato storm of the century is sailing around in luxury on the *Royal Caldera Forte* pretending to be the two of them?" The final few words of his question were only slightly lower in tone than the level of screaming, angry baby.

Cam opened his eyes "I'll be right there."

"And?"

"And I'll bring Ria along with me, of course. Do not tell anyone anything until I get there."

"As if. You'd better hurry it up, Cam. One of the possible illnesses Gage's med techs brought up is crust-fish fever."

Space potato storm. "Is it…that?" Cam asked. That would be bad. Really bad. Worst-case scenario bad.

"I don't know. No one seems to. They've narrowed it to that and a couple of other things. However, they are prepared to give her the first round of medicine if the green facial spots appear. But maybe it's something simple and she'll be on the mend soon. However, this will all be out of my control once she wakes up and is properly identified."

"Axel."

"What?"

"Thanks for—" he paused, not wanting to say out loud all the foolish things he'd already done in the name of love. "—you know."

His brother sounded weary. "Yeah. Sure. Whatever. Just get here. Because you know that the bad news is they may have to call a quarantine to keep it from spreading. And the worse news is Prudence's aunt, a Mrs. Virginia Westfall and one of the cousins are already showing the same signs of whatever this is."

"We're on our way." Cam shut his communicator off and looked at Ria.

"What's wrong?" she asked. "It sounds serious."

"I'm not certain where to start."

Cam scooted off the bed and Ria followed. "Start at the beginning."

"Your mother's lady's maid, Prudence, is currently in the basement medical facility very ill, unconscious, actually, with a possible case of crust-fish fever. They are standing by ready to give her the medication whenever the green spots show up, if they do. After that, she'll be awake in no time. We need to be there before she wakes up.

"Because crust-fish fever is so highly contagious for Alphas, the word quarantine has already been used. And to make matters even worse, Prudence's aunt, Mrs. Westfall and one of her cousins, are showing signs of whatever this is."

"Sounds like worst-case scenario already."

"Yep. Let's go."

Ria followed Cam out of the bedroom, through the living room and outside for one last quick look at the view. He had a nervous feeling in his belly for the first time since about age eight and learning what truly being in bad trouble meant.

They both got in his vehicle without a word, but once belted in, Ria asked the obvious question blaring big red warning klaxons in his head. The one Axel had already figured out. "So, wait a minute. If Prudence is in the basement with her aunt and cousins, who's been on the *Royal Caldera Forte* for the past week?"

"My brother Axel and I would both like to know the answer to that question. I'll put you down on the list at third."

"Oh." She looked worried.

"And my very clever brother has also finally recognized you from the picture your mother gave us."

"Oh no."

"Oh, yes. I knew he'd figure it out eventually, but I was hoping for much later." Cam stopped just past the gate and hopped out to close and lock it behind the SUV.

"On a scale of one to ten, how much trouble am I in?"

"If we were strangers and I was in charge, it would be a minimum of twenty."

"Since Axel is in charge, how much?" she said as one corner of her mouth lifted.

"Nineteen," he said in all seriousness. "If there is an outbreak of crust-fish fever in Alienn, lots of folks will be asking why Prudence was on Earth and not on the cruise ship."

"If she's sick, she would have gotten sick on the cruise ship, too."

He shook his head. "Except that all cruise liners from Alpha-Prime have built-in ventilation systems to identify infectious diseases at the earliest detection level and quash them before they become a problem. Prudence being in Alienn when she shouldn't have been, thereby possibly infecting all of the people she's had contact with in town with her highly contagious green-spotted rash disease, is something that could have been prevented if she'd only been where she was supposed to be."

"Space potato storm," Ria said under her breath.

"Exactly."

Chapter 15

Ria closed her eyes against the problems they faced because of her bucket list and need to be free from a future she didn't want. It wasn't fair, but no one ever said life was supposed to be. The weight of her guilt increased with each mile closer they drove to Alienn. A cacophony of what-ifs filled her mind. Maybe she'd get out of this arranged marriage because she'd be brought up on penal—possibly even gulag-level—charges for aiding and abetting the introduction of a dangerous contagion on a colony planet that had been disease-free since its inception.

Cam got them to the Big Bang Truck Stop quickly. The mid-morning sun shone brightly in the light-blue sky. Ria held his hand as they descended into the basement, Cam leading her through a maze of hallways and rooms until they came to an area that held several offices.

Axel shot out of the center door as they entered the passage. "Finally."

She barely knew him, and even she could see

his intense agitation at the prospect of a widespread outbreak of crust-fish fever. She didn't blame him. To his credit, he didn't give her a dirty look or anything. In fact, he looked relieved to see them.

Cam said, "Is it crust-fish fever for certain?"

Axel shook his head. "They don't know what it is. If it was, the green spots would have appeared by now."

"What does that mean?"

"Gage and the others are talking about cellular mutations and say maybe this is something we've never seen before. Whatever it is, it must have come off the cruise liner. Right?"

"Not necessarily. Don't borrow trouble."

"Your middle name is Trouble."

Cam rolled his eyes. "No, it's not. It's Zebulon, just like you and *all* of our brothers."

"Your middle name is Zebulon?" Ria smiled, trying for levity. "Good to finally get *that* important information."

Cam started to roll his eyes again, but winked at her instead. She couldn't help responding with a goofy grin.

The interplay appeared to amuse Axel, who divided a sly grin between his brother and Ria. The grin faded. "I haven't told Diesel, yet."

"Why not?"

Axel shrugged. "Mostly because he wasn't here earlier when I found out, but also because I wanted to talk to you about how this should be handled. This is more in your wheelhouse, yes?"

"Yes." Cam closed his eyes and tilted his head back as if thinking through a weighty problem. Ria figured she was the largest problem he faced and her guilt settled back on her shoulders heavier than ever.

"I'll tell him," she said. "This is all my fault anyway. I caused all of this by leaving the ship without permission."

Axel nodded slowly in understanding, but Cam's head snapped forward, his eyes popped open and she fell silent under the furious shock in his gaze. "No. Absolutely not. This isn't your fault." His hand tightened on hers while he brushed his fingers along her cheek, and whispered, "I'm glad you escaped the ship to check off your bucket list."

Axel's brows furrowed. "Seriously, Cam? Who are you and what have you done with my brother?"

"Shut it, Axel," he said, staring deeply into Ria's eyes with the warmest look of love and understanding she'd ever witnessed. A look she held and cherished, but she didn't deserve it.

"I love you, Cam, but it's time for me to…well, face the music."

"I disagree."

Axel said, "Does anyone care what I think?"

Cam's emphatic, "No," almost drowned out Ria's, "Sure. What do you think?"

"I really like her, Cam," Axel said, then startled when two workers passed them in an intersecting corridor. Lowering his voice, he said, "Let's move to a quieter place."

He gestured for them to go into the office he'd come out of. His name was stenciled on the door over the words, Chief of Communication. When they didn't move fast enough for his liking, he crowded behind them, practically stepping on their heels in his effort to herd them inside. Equipment, some of it familiar to Ria, more of it less so, filled the shelves in tidy rows.

Shutting the door, Axel said to Cam, "So, here's what we'll do. The two of us can go assess the situation, see if anything has changed and decide the best course of action. Ria can hide out in my office, so no one will know she's here."

Ria nodded. "He's right. I've never met Prudence's family, but they may have seen me in pictures." She shrugged. "I should stay out of sight."

"Aside from that," Axel said, "we don't have so many people working here that they won't notice a new Alpha wandering around. If anyone sees you with us, they might assume you're a new employee, but then they'd also expect us to introduce you."

"And when we didn't, that would only fuel their curiosity. Any chance of containing speculation about you would be nil," Cam said. "We'll be as quick as we can, Ria."

Cam kissed her hard, hugged her harder and then he and Axel left her to her own devices. Aside from the organized shelves of equipment, his walls featured several interesting drawings and a painting. Ria occupied herself studying them. The moniker W. Grey graced the lower right corner of each piece. *Must be another brother.*

A clock on Axel's desk helped her track how long they had been gone. After five minutes, she ran out of things to look at. She sat on Axel's small two-person sofa, then got up and paced for another five minutes. The clock seemed to tick the time by very slowly. Maybe it was broken.

Just when she was about to go stir crazy after less than twelve minutes alone, the door opened. A large figure, head down as he studied a sheaf of papers in his hand, spoke as he closed the door with a firm click. "Axel—" He looked up.

Ria felt the blood drain from her cheeks as she stared at Diesel.

"Pardon me," he said in an amused tone. "Where's Axel?"

She opened her mouth. Before she could say a word, his eyes narrowed suspiciously. "Wait. Weren't you with Cam at the Road Rash?"

Ria figured brazening it out was worth a try. She grinned, as if there was absolutely nothing wrong with the Fearless Leader finding her in Axel's office in the super-secret extraterrestrial facility under the Big Bang Truck Stop. "Yes. That was me."

Diesel nodded, pulled the Defender off his belt and pulled the trigger in one smooth motion. Ria gaped for a count of three, shocked at the speed with which he decided to shoot her and implemented that decision. Belatedly, she remembered she was supposed to be an earthling. "Oh," she said, trying to sound weary and drained. Even she thought she sounded unconvincing as she dropped to the floor with her eyes squeezed shut.

"Nice try," he said.

Ria remained where she was, flattening her lips, smashing her lids down even harder.

"I know you're awake."

She was about to burst. For some foolish reason, she held her breath when she landed on the floor. Now it was too late to try to breathe normally without gasping. Stupid.

"Your lips are turning blue. At least breathe in and out. Unconscious people do it all the time."

Ria released a long breath and sucked in enough air to say, "Fine. You've found me out. Are you happy?" She opened her eyes, expecting to see Cam's intimidating brother scowling down. He wore an engaging grin.

"I'm overjoyed, in fact." Diesel offered her a hand. She took it and he pulled her to her feet.

Completely baffled by his reaction, she watched him warily. "Thanks."

He nodded and crossed his arms comfortably, as if settling in for pleasant chat. "What's your story?"

"Well," she said ruefully. "It's a long one."

"I've got time."

Ria surprised herself. She thought she had more self-control. Well, no, she didn't, but she should when the situation was this dire. After keeping various guilt-inducing secrets throughout her illicit vacation on Earth, she unleashed a torrent of words that revealed everything. Absolutely everything.

She started with the odious arranged marriage to Dirt Bag FitzOsbern, moved along to meeting Cam at the earthling karaoke bar—she did, thankfully, manage to delicately gloss over what happened between that evening and the next morning in Cam's bed—told Diesel about missing the ship and how she and Cam had been busily going about adding items to her bucket list and crossing them off.

She finished her stream of consciousness tirade by sincerely expressing her unshakable true love for Cam, her devastation over the impossibility of any future for them, and her fear and guilt regarding the worst-case scenario playing out with regard to a mysterious cellular mutation that could spell disaster for the Alpha colony on Earth. And it was all her fault for not wanting to face the fact of her stupid arranged marriage.

Diesel didn't interrupt. He listened attentively, face as passive as if he faced such craziness all the time. Perhaps he did. Maybe that's why he'd earned the role of Fearless Leader so young. He must have enduring patience to deal with what she considered a huge crisis full of unsolvable problems and the unfairness of the world in general.

"In conclusion, the best I can hope for is not to end up at gulag XkR-9 for my multitude of crimes against humanity and Alpha-dom." Ria, exhausted by her verbal litany, plopped down on the small sofa and settled her hands on her knees. She pushed out a long, forlorn sigh.

Diesel surprised her by sitting next to her. He took one hand between his large, warm palms and patted it. "I don't think you'll end up at XkR-9, if that's any comfort."

"I'll take it," she said with a wan smile.

"Do you know who got aboard the *Royal Caldera Forte* in your place?"

"Not a clue. Until today, I believed it was Prudence Westfall, the lady's maid for my mother and either her aunt or one of her cousins. I don't suppose you know who it is?"

Diesel smiled, but not in a happy way. "Although my brothers have done a pretty good job of trying to keep me in the dark, I have a pretty good idea. The more I think about it, the more I'm convinced I'm right."

"Really? You should tell Cam and Axel because they didn't seem to have any idea when they left."

He patted the top of her hand again, released it and stood up. "Good idea. I'll go hunt them down.

You stay here. If you want, we can pretend this meeting never happened."

Ria shook her head. "I'm tired of pretending and tired of lying about what I'm doing all the time. I'm turning over a new leaf." Yet another cool Earther phrase. "I'm only telling the truth from now on."

Diesel tilted his head to one side. "Keep in mind that should you end up living here on Earth with Cam—"

"I doubt that'll ever be possible."

"—you'll have to hide the fact you're an Alpha from any and all earthlings. No exceptions."

"I understand, but I seriously doubt it will even be an issue. It would take a miracle."

"Don't discount miracles. They happen more often than you might imagine."

He left her to ponder her rather contrary thoughts on miracles.

The Defender had done absolutely nothing to drain her of energy. The same couldn't be said of her wrenching confession to Diesel. She sagged against the back of the sofa. Curling her legs up beside her, she propped one elbow on the arm and cradled her chin in her palm. Her eyelids felt unbelievably heavy. She wondered what magic it would take to produce the miracle she so desperately needed. Thoughts of Cam and how wonderful it would be to stay with him on Earth, building a life together on the beautiful slice of paradise he'd shared with her just a few short hours ago, followed her into sleep.

Cam hated leaving Ria alone in Axel's office, but the moment they got to the medical wing and spoke to Gage, he was glad she didn't have to hear about it. Even the worst-case scenario of a crust-fish fever epidemic was better than an unknown pathogen on the loose. And as far as how the possible mutation might impact the human population traipsing through the Big Bang Truck Stop? Catastrophic-case scenario.

Gage met them at the entrance to the medical wing. "Cam, I'm glad you're here. I wish I had better news."

"Still no change?"

"Oh no. There have been lots of changes. Two members of Prudence's family, her aunt, Virginia Westfall and one of her cousins, Claire, are exhibiting the same symptoms. The other cousin, Cindy has no symptoms whatsoever. And that's the only good news."

"And the bad?"

"The Westfall family's next door neighbor, Mr. Barbour, an Alpha man our father's age, has come down with the same thing."

Axel sucked in an audible breath as they followed their brother through the entrance into the deserted reception area. "It's spreading?"

Gage shrugged. "It must be. I don't know what this illness is, but that is my first assumption based on all we know. And I use the word 'all' very loosely, since we don't know much."

"What about the cousin who isn't sick?"

"At first, she had the same symptoms as the others. Over the course of a couple hours, she got better. She never lost consciousness, but she's sound asleep now, clearly physically exhausted. It's like her body needs to recharge. We could try to force her awake with meds, but the consensus is she should sleep until she wakes on her own. Unfortunately, that means I haven't been able to question her."

"Does Diesel know yet?" Axel asked the question, but Cam wanted to know the answer more.

"I called him. He's on his way down."

Cam's first inclination was to get back to Ria and avoid a confrontation with Diesel in his capacity as Fearless Leader, but he planted his feet, prepared to answer for the consequences of this debacle of epic proportions.

Gage told Axel, "I caught him as he was leaving your office, so he should be here shortly."

A line of icy fear ran down Cam's spine. He and Axel exchanged a quick and intense death stare of *what in the space potato world of debauchery* could go more wrong?

As if conjured, Diesel appeared at the entryway.

"Gage, Axel." He pinned his chief of security with an unbending gaze that shouted, "I know exactly what you've done," and said, "*Cam*."

Not one of the three younger brothers missed his tone.

"What's going on down here, Gage? Why the urgent call?" He stared at Cam as he spoke.

Cam refused to be intimidated. He'd screwed up, but he wasn't a child. "Were you just in Axel's office?" He couldn't help himself. The world was caving in around him, but he needed to know what, if any, interaction Diesel had had with Ria.

"Maybe. Why?"

"You know why."

Diesel crossed his arms. Cam recognized his eldest brother's stance. It was the one he used when preparing to deliver a lecture. "What if I told you I ran into someone unexpected in Axel's office?"

Cam shrugged.

"And what if I told you I shot that person with a Defender?"

"Infantile revenge isn't really your style, but whatever helps you get through the day." Cam mirrored Diesel's stance. He hoped Ria was okay. He was glad they'd talked about what she should do if someone pointed a Defender at her. Diesel wasn't one for leaving loose ends, so he'd probably rounded up someone to move the "unconscious"

Ria aboveground so she would "wake up" there without any memory of the underground facilities.

"Why would you shoot her with a Defender?" Axel asked. "She's an Alpha."

Cam shot Axel a glare.

"She is?" Diesel said with a sly smile. Axel's revelation was obviously not news to him. "Where on Earth did she come from?"

Axel shot Cam an apologetic look.

Cam cleared his throat. "That's one problem, Diesel. She didn't come from anywhere on Earth. She came from Alpha-Prime on the *Royal Caldera Forte* and got left behind."

"Don't they do a fairly extensive and rigorous count on the cruise ships, especially the *Royal Caldera Forte*? Gotta keep track of all those rich people."

"You'd think. But that's only one of many problems we are trying to hash out right now. Join us, why don't you?"

Diesel nodded. "I'd love to. So, here is what I bring to the table. I believe I know exactly who is aboard the ship due back in two days."

"Who?" Cam and Axel said in unison. They punched each other and played the jinx game as if by habit.

Cam shouldn't be surprised that Diesel seemed to be entirely aware of the situation, despite their best efforts to keep it from him. On top of that, his quick mind had ferreted out some answers to questions that had baffled Cam. That was why Diesel was their Fearless Leader.

"Who is the only person or persons missing from Alienn in the past week?" Diesel asked pointedly.

Cam shrugged. "I don't know. Who?"

Diesel shook his head pityingly. "That's right. You've been too busy off playing with your new blue-haired Alpha girlfriend to notice the unnatural quiet that has descended on the Big Bang Truck Stop this week."

Axel's eyes widened and his mouth dropped open. "Good grief. Aunt Dixie?"

Diesel nodded. "And I expect that her cohort in crime is Miss Penny. Surely you all know Miss Penny's talents as a descendent of Alpha-Prime's fabled shifter race. She can take the form of anyone for short periods of time. Our two elderly troublemakers have likely sequestered themselves inside Ria's luxury quarters. All Miss Penny would have to do is take on the form of Prudence or Ria and stick her head out the door a couple of times a day to keep everyone at bay.

"They may even be feigning illness and having food and luxuries brought to their room."

Cam felt exasperated with himself for not figuring it out. Granted, he had been paying more attention to Ria than anything else. "All Miss Penny would have to say is that she's meeting with Ria's dirt bag future fiancé and I'm certain her mother would leave her alone."

"Wait. Ria has a dirt bag future fiancé?" Axel asked, shock coloring his tone.

"Unfortunately, yes, there is another foolish arranged marriage in the mix, if you can believe it."

"What happens next?" Axel asked.

"Okay, the good news—and I can't believe I'm saying this—is that if Aunt Dixie and Miss Penny are aboard the cruise liner, it's really one less thing we have to worry about," Diesel said.

"Why?" Cam didn't quite follow his brother's train of thought.

"Do you believe for a moment that if either of them have been discovered, Director Patmore wouldn't have sent a message back condemning us all to the boiling, dark side of the Lava Rock World for punishment by now?"

"Good point," Axel said. "I'm sure Aunt Dixie would follow all the rules in this singular event to ensure she isn't found out. The moment she gets caught is the moment we hear about it and she has to face us upon her return."

Diesel nodded. "But if she can keep her cool for a whole ten days, no one will ever know she was gone or what she was doing."

"Right," Axel said. "Ria can simply slip back onto the cruise liner for the return to Alpha-Prime." The moment the words came out of his mouth, he slid Cam another apologetic look. "Sorry, Cam."

Cam shrugged. "I know that's a possible outcome, but Ria wants to try to talk her mother into letting her out of the arranged marriage to stay here with me."

Axel made an odd noise, like a snort or a muffled sneeze. "This is the same woman we spoke to, right? The one who in no uncertain terms let us know Alexandria is set to marry Douglass Bernard FitzOsbern, of the Technician Class FitzOsberns? La-di-dah."

"That's the one. But Ria doesn't love him. She doesn't want to marry him. She calls him Dirt Bag FitzOsbern. Apparently, he feels the same way about marrying her." Cam hated even thinking of Ria being with anyone else, ever.

Diesel nailed it on the head by saying, "No one likes arranged marriages except for parents trying to get thirtysomething-plus deadbeat kids out of their houses so they can retire and live the good life."

"Like our parents puttering around the country in an RV like retired humans." Axel looked at the ceiling.

"Exactly," Diesel said.

"Doesn't help if her mother won't agree to negate the arrangement, and she won't." Cam knew Ria's mother would not relent.

"Because?" Diesel asked.

"Because her late husband didn't leave her enough funds to live the way she wants and the marriage contract includes a generous stipend for Ria's mother after the nuptials."

An alarm blared to life.

"Now what?" Cam wondered at his capacity to take in more bad news.

"That's the medical alarm, isn't it?" Axel asked no one in particular.

Gage looked at his communication device and spat out a colorful swear word. To his brothers, he said, "Someone opened a vent they shouldn't have."

Diesel asked, "Is the virus loose in the way station?"

He looked up, his expression miserable. "No. Worse."

"What's worse than that?"

"The med lab where the patients have been quarantined was vented to the outside of the station, right next to the gas pumps."

Nova, Diesel's assistant, burst into the reception area. Her flushed cheeks and wild eyes said she'd sprinted all the way down from Diesel's upstairs office at the back of the truck stop's convenience store. "Come quick!" Between gasps, she said, "Upstairs. The humans." Their eyes followed her pointing finger to the truck stop above them.

A sickening feeling shot to Cam's belly. "What about the humans upstairs?"

"They are sick or something."

"Sick?" *No!* "What kind of sick?" Cam started moving toward the nearest exit up to ground level, his brothers right behind him.

"Don't know. I think it might be bad." Nova, hand on her chest as she labored to breathe, kept pace. "They're dropping like flies in the parking lot and out by the gas pumps."

She sounded like she was about to cry.

Grimly, Gage said, "You all go ahead. I need to go back and round up a medical team. If there's any chance we can help the humans, we'll need to act fast."

"Do it," Diesel said.

Cam took the stairs two at a time. If the accidental venting had spread the mysterious illness to the earthlings and it was so virulent it affected them almost instantaneously, this problem was catastrophic on a level he wasn't sure the way station could recover from.

Chapter 16

"Five are down that I saw," Nova reported as they reached ground level and hurried to the front of the convenience store. "A car drove in as four people hit the ground. The driver jumped out to help and immediately got taken down by whatever affected the other humans. He must have forgotten to put the car in Park, because it rolled and took out several stacks of a brand-new shipment at Satellite Tire. Snow tires rolled everywhere, including onto the highway…"

Cam stopped short of the door and stared outside. A disturbing stillness characterized the chaotic scene. Black rubber circles dotted the area. A newer model car, engine still running, driver's door ajar, butted up against a diminished stack of tires beside Satellite Tire. A man lay facedown between the pumps and Satellite Tire, and Cam guessed he was the driver who'd tried to help. An SUV and a compact, gas nozzles stuck in the tanks, waited beside the pumps. A woman in capris and a halter top slumped beside the compact's front end, head to chest and squeegee still held in one hand. Three other humans could be seen from where he stood.

He hoped they were only unconscious.

Cam reached for the door. Diesel pulled him back. "What are you doing?"

"Going outside."

"What if you go down, too?"

"Then you'll know whatever it is affects Alphas, too."

"No."

"No?"

"I'm not risking you as an experiment. We need to take the time to assess the situation before anyone goes outside."

He knew his brother was right, but he didn't have to like it. "Fine."

The three brothers, Nova trailing Diesel, spread out along the front of the store to get different vantage points.

Cam glanced at the counter, then did a double-take. The cashier, a skinny kid with a mop of dark hair, faced away from the counter. Huddled in the corner, he held a phone receiver with a white-knuckled hand and spoke in a low but urgent tone, ignoring the mayhem in the lot. He looked over his shoulder, saw the Grey brothers, and flinched. He said something hurriedly into the receiver and hung up.

Cam saw the problem immediately. He wasn't

sure if he should just be grateful or put a hand on his chest to keep his heart from leaping outside his body in supreme relief.

"Hold on," he called out to Diesel and Axel. "They aren't down because of the venting."

"How do you know?" Diesel asked.

Wordlessly, he pointed at the kid's hip. Diesel and Axel moved toward the counter.

"Space potatoes. What an idiot." Axel pushed out a breath.

"Carl!" Diesel called out rather loudly.

The kid came to attention like a soldier under orders. The movement jostled the Defender strapped at his waist, freeing it and the jammed-on trigger from the edge of the counter.

Cam could have kicked himself. He'd never considered a trigger guard. The wheels started spinning in his head that perhaps he needed to add the feature to the next Defender upgrade.

"What?" Carl asked, sounding defensive. He seemed angry over the interruption to his phone call.

"Why do you have a Defender strapped to your hip?"

Even a flinty-toned Diesel didn't seem to scare this kid. "We always keep a Defender behind the counter here for emergencies."

"That's not what I asked." Diesel confiscated the Defender and looked at the controls. He pointed outside. "Look what you just did."

Grudgingly, the kid looked at the gas pumps. His teenage insolence fell away and he gaped at the spectacle of fallen humans and rubber tires dotting the lot like daisies in a field.

"It's set for ten minutes," Diesel said. "At a guess, I'd say we've already lost at least five. We're going to have to work fast to make sure no one's hurt and get everyone back in place."

The brothers looked up at the sound of running feet from the rear of the store. Gage and a team of six, all wearing containment suits and carrying med kits, crowded in from the office corridor.

"False alarm, Gage," Diesel called out. "They were all downed by a Defender. We'll need all hands on deck to help clear up the mess, though, before they wake up."

"You got it, Diesel. My team can stay to help while I get back to our patients."

Axel raced outside. He carefully checked over the first patron he came to, seeing no injuries. He put the guy back inside his SUV as Cam and one of Gage's techs did the same for the young couple—one half of which was the woman with the squeegee—on the other side of the pump station. Two tire store employees raced out to get the driver of the car that had taken out their tires. They pushed the vehicle toward the pumps and parked it behind the couple's compact as if he was waiting in line. It wasn't perfect, but they did what they had to do. Protecting their secret was paramount.

The last patron was an older Alpha with a cane. He'd dropped it when he fell. Cam worried about broken bones, but the guy was awake by the time they got to him. Ed owned Satellite Tire.

"Sorry," he said. "I tripped over my own gol-durn feet racing over here when I saw the tires rolling onto the highway."

Cam blew out a breath of relief. "Not your fault, Ed."

"Did Carl have the Defender strapped to his hip again?"

"How'd you know?"

"He's done it before. I told him he shouldn't, but those young whippersnappers never listen to old man wisdom."

His brothers, Carl and Gage's suited-up team members began to round up scattered tires and return them to neat stacks beside Ed's shop.

"Next time you see something, call me."

"I'm not a tattletale, Cam."

"It's not tattling when it comes to the colony's safety." Cam helped Ed stand, quickly changing the subject from wayward truck-stop employees. "I've never seen you with a cane." Alphas rarely needed aid like this. They had healing abilities. Was Ed sick? Being affected differently by whatever was going on downstairs?

"It's only temporary. I broke my gol-durn ankle a couple of days ago and my healing is just slow."

"Slow?"

He nodded. "Getting old isn't for sissies, young man. Alphas aren't immune to age and all that comes with it. They get slower in their twilight years, too, just like the humans."

"No doubt."

"And I know what you're thinking. Why don't I just go on home to Alpha-Prime like every second Alpha old timer here?"

"Not what I was thinking at all, Ed." *Maybe a little.* "I have no doubt you'll recover and be back to your old self again in no time."

"The thing is, I've been alone now for a quite a while. Lately, I've reconsidered having a romance in my later years."

Ed? Romance? Cam absolutely did *not* want to discuss romance and all it entailed with the senior. *How can I change the subject?*

He nudged Ed, nodding at the pump area. The humans were waking up. The other Alphas hadn't managed to gather all the rogue tires. He didn't know how he'd explain the mess. Strong wind gust? *Maybe*. Mini tornado? *Possibly*. Act of nature? *Another possibility*. Alien Defender technology issue? *No, absolutely not*. Maybe no one would ask.

Ed cleared his throat, leaned close and whispered, "Do you think your aunt Dixie is looking for a sweetheart?"

Cam was so focused on the earthlings it took a couple of seconds to realize what Ed had asked.

"What?" The world around him fell away as the

idea of Aunt Dixie romantically involved with Ed the Tire Man circulated in his head. *Would it be better? Could it be worse?* What if Aunt Dixie had a boyfriend? Maybe she'd be distracted and wouldn't cause as much trouble. Hmm.

"Is she seeing anybody?" Ed asked as if fearful of the answer.

"I honestly don't know. I haven't seen her with anyone."

"Would you put in a good word for me?"

"Of course, Ed, I'd be happy to. Aunt Dixie would be lucky to have you."

"Aces. Thanks, my boy."

"Sure thing." Cam would have to share this tidbit with his brothers. They could discuss the pros and cons of a romance between Aunt Dixie and their neighbor. Axel approached, wiping the back of his hand over a brow shiny with sweat from slinging tires.

Nova came running outside. She was out of breath again. "Come downstairs. Bad news. Bad."

Now what?

"Now what?" Axel said, echoing Cam's thought.

Nova motioned urgently.

Diesel told his brothers, "You go. I'll follow after I clean up this mess." A couple of the earthlings seemed puzzled to find themselves where they were. Diesel was the best one to deal with the fallout from Carl's accidental Defender use.

Nova led them directly to Gage just outside the

double silver doors to the medical zone where they'd quarantined Prudence and her relatives.

"Bad news," he said. "Now the neighbor across the street from the Westfall's home has also come down with the same illness. He called for help. They brought him in while you were dealing with the situation up top."

"It's spreading further?" Easygoing Axel looked more worried than Cam had ever seen him.

Gage shrugged. "That's what it looks like."

Axel turned to Cam. "We'll have to send a team to the aunt's house."

"I'll go." Cam blamed himself. If only he had turned Ria in immediately upon discovering her identity. If only she weren't so beautiful and perfect for him. If only he hadn't fallen in love at first sight. If, if, if didn't do him any good since he couldn't have done anything different. At no point did turning her in seriously cross his mind.

"You're on vacation. And contrary to what I *know* you're thinking right now, this isn't your fault." Axel put a hand on Cam's shoulder.

"Sure it is. The moment I saw the picture her mother gave us, I should have turned her in."

Axel frowned. "But you love her."

"I do, but that's beside the point. I broke the rules. A cardinal rule, in fact, and now we're all paying the price for it."

"Love isn't beside the point, Cam, it *is* the point," Axel said fiercely. "If you find someone you love, and that person feels the same way, nothing—especially a stupid arranged marriage—should stand in your way."

"I didn't know you felt this way."

A strange smile shaped Axel's mouth. "Well, I may have watched the two of you for a while before I rudely interjected myself into your moment at the mall. She loves you. You love her. It's so obvious a blind person could see it. Love like that should never be considered wrong or inconvenient. It would be the height of foolishness to turn someone you love in because of a rule, cardinal or not. I know things look dire, but have faith. Eventually it will all work out."

Cam appreciated Axel's optimism. He took a deep breath and exhaled, trying to dislodge the panic that was growing inside him at an exponential rate. He was grateful his brother could see the love he and Ria shared, but it wouldn't make any difference in the end. Ria was trapped in an arranged marriage, and beyond the crazy notion of faking her death—which probably wouldn't work anyway—he didn't know how to free her.

With this mysterious illness running rampant in town—caused possibly by the lady's maid coming ashore to find Ria—it was only a matter of time before the facts surfaced and they would be ruined. At best, his job here on Earth would be stripped from him and he'd be sent back to Alpha-Prime, separated from his family forever. At worst, he faced a quick trip to a gulag to serve hard time, breaking boulders into pea gravel with a sledgehammer until the day he died.

He would gladly take the fall for Ria, even if it meant dying in a gulag. But it hurt more than he could fathom that saving her would force her into a future with someone else.

He almost hoped for the gulag. If he was sent to Alpha-Prime, he'd be forced to witness her future life with another man, a dirt bag, no less. That was the very definition of hard time.

Ria woke on Axel's sofa refreshed and ready to do battle. If her mother had been near, she would have sought her out and explained her feelings. As she wasn't, Ria waited impatiently for Cam or Axel or anyone to return. She gathered some courage and cracked open Axel's office door to peek out. She saw nothing and no one. She opened the door wider. No one was around. There was not a sound nearby.

She stepped from the room, closed Axel's office door and tiptoed down the hall until she reached the lounge where the cruise liner's passenger had disembarked.

There were a few people in the large space that was described in the way station literature as a small town-sized area of fun. Ria skirted the edge, making her way toward the stairs leading up and out. She climbed the staircase, noting it looked different from the previous escape route she'd used. At the top of the stairs, she opened a door—and heard voices.

She crept down the hall. As she got closer, she recognized the speakers as Cam and Axel.

Cam said something like, "I didn't know you felt this way."

An air vent came alive beside her, muffling the first part of Axel's response. She had to move closer to catch, "...it would be the height of foolishness to turn someone you love in because of a rule, cardinal or not. I know things look dire, but have faith. Eventually it will all work out."

Cam loved her? That was good. He was thinking about turning her in? That wasn't so good. She couldn't blame him, though. This whole fiasco was her fault, starting with her bucket list and all she'd done to thumb her nose at the rules.

Ria knew only one thing: She wouldn't let him suffer because of her. If it came down to it and there was no other choice, he couldn't turn her in if she turned herself in.

"What are you doing there?"

A small scream escaped before she could stop it and Ria jumped a foot off the ground. She turned to see a stranger.

Her eyes dropped to the woman's name tag and she said, "Hi, Nova."

The woman ignored her friendly tone to say, "Who are you?"

"I'm a friend of Cam's."

Her brows furrowed. "How do you know my name?"

Ria pointed to her name tag.

The woman rolled her eyes and flashed a quick smile. "Forgive my rudeness. It's been quite a day and I've just had too much excitement."

Cam and Axel must have heard Ria's scream, because they were right there, Cam demanding, "Are you okay? I heard you scream."

"I'm fine." She launched into his arms, kissed his mouth and said, "I won't let you get into trouble over what I did."

"What did you do?" Nova asked. The eager look in her wide eyes said louder than the words that she couldn't wait to get a taste of possible gossip.

"Nothing," Axel and Cam said. As Ria had come to expect, they punched each other and said, "Jinx!" The punching was likely their favorite part.

"I tried to escape an arranged marriage," Ria said over their brotherly scuffle.

Nova frowned. "Gracious me, who hasn't? I thought you were going to say something interesting." She marched away, mumbling something about a withering grapevine in the greater township of Alienn.

Cam hugged Ria, sending her attention to his troubled face.

"Did it turn out to be crust-fish fever?" she asked.

"No."

"That's good, right?"

Axel shook his head. "Unfortunately, it's worse. Now they think it's a mutation. They aren't quite sure because no one has ever seen anything like it before."

Cam seemed lost in thought. Axel nudged him with an elbow. "What should we do? Give me a direction and I'll go."

"I might have an idea," Cam said. "I've been working on a device that can detect certain dangerous substances. It's a prototype, but I've tested it on a dozen or so common things. It might not tell us exactly what this is, but could identify whether something was toxic to Alphas."

"Brilliant!"

Cam began walking, arm around Ria. His brother started to follow, but Cam turned abruptly. "Axel, go fetch Jack. We'll send him in."

"Jack," Ria asked. "Who's Jack?"

Axel said, "Jack is our up-for-anything brother. He's the youngest of us, and we used to torture him the most. That's probably why now he just volunteers for everything."

"Suit him up," Cam said.

Axel flipped off a casual salute. "Will do. Meet you in your lab, yes?"

"Yes. I need to make a few adjustments on the device, but it shouldn't take long."

Axel jogged away. Cam took Ria's hand and led her to a door with another code box. He punched in the same number he'd used at the cabin. She tried not to look, but couldn't help herself. If he didn't want her to know, he should have hidden it better.

The door buzzed and popped open. She followed him into a large room with several tables covered in all manner of mechanical and technical-looking devices. All four walls were lined floor to ceiling with shelves holding a variety of books and supplies any alien mad scientist would be delighted to own. The overhead lights were as bright as daylight.

Ria stared around with interest. "I've been dying to see your lab, Cam."

"Have you?" He sounded distracted as he searched the first table. None of the several small devices on it appeared to be what he was looking for. He moved to another table that held even more gadgets, eventually picking up a gray rectangular item about the size of a shoebox. It had a screen, two dials and several buttons. A silver antenna sprouted out the top.

He carried the device to a third table. This one looked more like a workspace, as room had been kept clear for a desktop computer, papers and tools. Cam took the cover off the box. Inside, lots of little working parts, lights, diodes, circuit boards and wires went in every which direction.

"What is that again?" Ria watched him use a

tiny straight tool to twist and poke around his invention's innards.

"Hmmm? Oh. An Alpha poison detector for both physical and gaseous substances."

He didn't stop what he was doing and barely seemed aware of her presence. He was definitely in his element. All he needed was a lab coat and a clipboard and he'd look like every scientist she'd ever seen, real or on broadcast videos. He was focused. He was talented. He was perfect.

Ria wanted a life with him so much, tears threatened to spill over her lids. She had to think of something else.

Since he was absorbed in his work, Ria left him to look around his laboratory, surreptitiously swiping at her eyes so he wouldn't think she was a big crybaby.

She'd been impressed to find out Cam was the inventor everyone on Alpha-Prime was talking about, thanks to the Defender technology. The controlled chaos of his lab proved the Defender wasn't his only brilliant idea. He had a busy, inquiring, fascinating mind.

And Ria was in love with him.

"Okay, that's it." Cam put his tool down and snapped the top back on the shoebox.

As he did, Axel and a guy dressed in a white suit, white helmet tucked under one arm, entered the lab. The newcomer definitely bore the Grey genes. There would be no mistaking him for anyone but a close relative of Cam, Axel and Diesel.

Axel performed the introductions. "Ria, this is our youngest brother, Jack." He turned to the younger man. "Jack, this is Cam's new girlfriend, Ria."

"Cam has a girlfriend? That really *is* new," Jack said with a grin, reaching out his hand to shake hers like all Earthers did. Ria was getting good at shaking hands.

"What is it you want me to do again?" Jack asked.

Cam handed him the gray shoebox. "We want you to go check out the house of a possible poison victim."

"Poison victim?" he said warily. "What poison?"

"That's why we're sending you in with this device, to find out."

"Got it." He took the box from Cam.

Cam quickly gave Jack the rundown on how to operate the device. "This white button turns it on. The silver probe extension is what tests the air. This blue button will retrieve a sample of the air. Just push the blue button and wave it over the area you want to test. The results will show up on the screen as either toxic or non-toxic to Alphas."

"Will it tell me what the poison is?"

"Likely not. It will only register a few basic toxins. You'll have to bring the box back after you sample the entire house for a thorough report.

Axel, you drive. Take the van with the portable decontamination unit. Whatever you do, Jack, do *not* get in the cab of the van with Axel before your suit and the exterior of the device get the green-light from the unit, or we might wind up being down one brother. I'll monitor you through your helmet. When you get back, I'll plug the data port into my computer to determine the exact substance if you find anything that registers as toxic."

"Got it. I'm off to find the poison." Jack, helmet in one hand, device in the other, headed out of the lab with Axel.

Cam watched them go, then walked over and took Ria in his arms. He kissed her.

"I love you, Ria. I don't know what's going to happen, but I don't ever want to be without you."

Ria hugged him hard, searching her brain for anything that might help them stay together. She came up with nothing. Not a single thing. Tears again welled up in her eyes. This time, she let them fall. So what if she was a crybaby.

She sniffled, but then a measure of resolve straightened her spine.

When the ship docked the day after tomorrow, she'd talk to her mother. Whatever it took, she'd make her mother understand her feelings. She had to, because without Ruth Latham Borne changing her mind and calling off the arranged marriage, Ria and Cam were doomed.

Chapter 17

Cam leaned back from the hug when he heard Ria sniffle. "Don't cry. We'll figure something out."

"Like what?"

"I'm not sure, but I haven't even told you my worst-case scenario plan."

"Worst-case scenario plan?" She wiped her tears away with the heel of one hand and looked hopeful. "Tell me."

"I only thought of it about half an hour ago. I haven't worked out all the details yet."

"Tell me the basics. I need hope. Maybe I can help with the details."

He pushed out a long breath. "Well, you can't get married to Dirt Bag if everyone thinks you're dead."

Her eyes went wide. "*Dead?* Your idea is to take me out to prevent my arranged marriage?" She dropped her arms from him and took a step back, brows furrowed in confusion.

He couldn't help it. He laughed. "No. I'm not going to take you out, Ria. My idea is to *fake* your death."

Her lips formed a drawn-out, "Oh," before she moved back into his arms, resting her head on his shoulder. "Interesting idea."

"Like I said, it's my worst-case scenario plan. I don't know if it would work. I'm not even sure if we should try it. Ultimately, we'd have to disappear."

"I'd hate to take you away from your family."

"I'd do it for you." Cam pressed his face into her hair, inhaled deeply and memorized her wonderful scent.

Ria's arms tightened around him. "Let's hope it doesn't come to that."

Cam's communicator beeped. He took it off of his belt and read the text. "They're at the house. Jack is ready to go in and start testing." He moved back to his desk, tapped some keys. The computer monitor blipped to a clear image of a door. The image shifted left, then right, taking in a mailbox on one side and a small potted tree on the other.

Cam said, "Can you hear me, Jack?"

"Yep." The younger man's voice came through the speakers loud and clear.

"Go on in the front door. It should be unlocked. Take a reading as soon as you step inside."

On the monitor, Jack's gloved hand reached for the knob, turned it, and the door swung open. The view moved with Jack as he stepped inside and briefly looked back to close the door. He held the box up in view and pressed the blue button. The screen on the box registered the sample as non-toxic. *Good. Maybe it isn't airborne.*

"Where do I go next?" Jack took a few steps further into the house.

"Looks like you're in the living area. Go to the center of the room and take another sample."

"Okay." Jack took another sample, which also came up as non-toxic.

"Head for the kitchen. Test some stuff in the refrigerator. Maybe something is spoiled, but not visibly bad."

"Will do." Jack checked the entire kitchen area, but nothing came up toxic.

Cam noticed through Jack's helmet camera that the slider that led from the kitchen to the backyard was ajar. "Hey, Jack. Head outside. Maybe they grilled something."

Jack opened the slider and walked out onto the back deck.

Immediately, it was clear something had gone very wrong here. Six place settings had been laid out on the picnic table. Plates half-filled with food, a partial platter of some sort of grilled meat—chicken, maybe—BBQ beans, corn on the cob and an untouched pie in the center of the table now provided a grand feast for a cloud of flies and lines of marching ants.

The grill lid was closed, but smoke filtered from beneath the hood.

"Check the grill. Maybe they got some bad

chicken." Food poisoning was the best option at this point.

Jack opened the grill, exposing almost unrecognizable chunks of some kind of meat. The little lumps looked like charcoal on the grill, smoking and inedible, whatever it had once been. "Put the probe into one of the charred pucks and see if it's bad meat."

Jack pushed the button. As soon as the results flashed on the device's screen, Cam straightened in surprise.

"Squirrel?" Jack said. "They were eating squirrel? How is that even possible? Everyone knows squirrel meat is poisonous to Alphas."

They'd found that out the hard way. About eighty years back, early colonists figured they could chow down on whatever the locals did. They couldn't. Alphas couldn't tolerate squirrel meat, at all. It led to a slow, painful death if not treated early enough.

Beside him, Ria huffed. "Even *I* know squirrel meat is poisonous to Alphas, and I've known that since I was four years old."

"At least now we know why they're so sick," Jack said. "That just leaves, did they eat it willingly or was someone trying to kill off the whole family? Why would they all eat something they knew was poisonous?"

"No clue," Cam said. "But I'll tell Gage what we think it is so he can get started on their treatment."

Cam messaged Gage, who responded with incredulity, but indicated he'd start the regimen immediately.

"Can they recover?" Ria asked. "I always thought eating squirrel was a death sentence."

"It's very bad for the Alpha system, and eventually will kill whoever's fool enough to eat it, but it's not a fast-acting toxin. They are probably going to hurt for a long time, though."

Cam linked his fingers with Ria's and led her from his laboratory to the medical facility.

Again, Gage met them at the door. Cam smiled inwardly. He was supposed to be the security expert, always alert to everything in and around the way station, but Gage seemed to be preternaturally plugged in when it came to his own domain. "Prudence is awake," he reported. "Her eyes popped open the moment I gave her the antidote. I was just on my way to get you."

His eyes went to Ria.

Cam's fingers tightened on her slender hand. "Gage, this is Ria, the woman I love. Ria, my brother, Gage. He's the man in charge of our medical facilities, and responsible for the care your lady's maid and her family have been receiving." When Gage would have commented, Cam shook his head. "I'll explain in more detail later. Right now, just take us to Prudence."

"You got it."

Now that they knew the toxin had been

ingested, and wasn't an airborne issue, there was nothing to stop them from conversing directly with the patients. Cam needed to find out why they'd eaten something they knew was poisonous.

Prudence, a slender, middle-aged woman with shoulder length brown hair, looked drawn tucked into one of the med center's beds. She was awake, but obviously weak as she asked, "What happened to me?"

"You ingested poison," Cam said from the foot of her bed.

Her brows furrowed. "Poison? What kind of poison?"

At Gage's nod, Cam continued, "Who brought the meat to the house to grill?"

Prudence's eyes widened. Her eyes were on Ria, who stood at Cam's side. "Alexandria? Is that you?" The lady's maid looked suddenly very guilty. Cam guessed it was because she'd realized neither woman was supposed to be on Earth. He'd have to question her about that, as well, but first he needed to know why she'd eaten poison.

"Where did the meat that you grilled come from, Prudence?" Ria asked.

Prudence swallowed hard. "I bought it in a little town called Skeeter Bite." Her gaze shot to Cam. "I know I'm not supposed to be here. And I also know that I shouldn't have ventured so far from Alienn, but I wanted to see more of Earth."

Cam and Gage traded a look and frowned. "You bought squirrel meat?"

"No! I would never, ever get squirrel. It wasn't squirrel meat." She tried to sit up, but went pale with the effort.

Gage put a hand on her shoulder and gently pushed her back to the mattress. The bed was raised at an angle so she could talk. There was no reason for her to exert herself. "I was going to get some chicken, but the man said he was having a sale on something called varmint. He said it was kind of like chicken, but better. He called it a redneck delicacy. So I brought it home and we grilled it."

"And you didn't think to ask what varmint was?" Cam asked.

Prudence looked confused. "No. The better question is why that man would sell me squirrel meat. Doesn't he know Alphas are allergic to it?"

"No, I really hope not. If he was an Alpha, he never would have sold it to you. If he was a human, he shouldn't even *know* about Alphas. Unless you told him about us. Did you?"

She paled further. "No, of course not. I didn't tell him anything."

"Did you think it looked like squirrel meat?"

Her brow furrowed. "No, it looked like a small chicken. Tasted like chicken, too," she said under her breath. "Honestly, I know what a live squirrel looks like, but I've never seen one cut up and ready to grill." She looked at Cam. "This is probably a good lesson that Alpha-Prime should update its files on the Earth colony."

"I'll keep that in mind. One more thing: Did you invite two of your aunt's neighbors over to eat with you?"

"Yes. How did you...oh no—" She stopped talking abruptly. "Is anyone *dead*? Did I kill anyone?"

"No," Gage reassured her. "We just want to be sure we're treating anyone who may have been impacted."

"My cousin Cindy grilled a cow steak, but she did have one small bite of what we all thought was varmint."

Gage nodded. "That makes sense. One of your cousins wasn't as sick as the others."

"I'm so sorry. Honestly, I didn't know."

Cam figured everyone was well appraised about the few dangers on the Earth colony. "How long has your family lived here?"

"Not too long, a few months, maybe. My uncle was killed last year in an accident on Alpha-Prime, but he'd always talked about visiting Earth. My aunt wanted a fresh start, so she volunteered to work at the bauxite plant doing inventory."

"I have some other questions for you," Cam said. "Gage, can you leave us?"

"Why?"

"The less you know, the better. Trust me on this one."

Gage shook his head, visibly annoyed about being kept out of the loop, but left the room. "What made you stay behind on Earth?"

Prudence stared at her folded hands, then picked at the blanket on the bed as if she didn't want to answer. "I'd rather not say," she said quietly.

"I need to know."

Prudence looked at Ria. "Your mother sent me to find you. She thought perhaps you knew I had family here and went to visit them. I didn't think so, but I didn't tell her that. When I got to my aunt's house, she hadn't seen you, but one of her neighbors happened by, overheard what we were talking about and asked what you looked like. She went to her nephew's house to get him to help look for you. When she came back to my aunt's place, she said she saw you, but it didn't look like you wanted to leave. I'm not sure why she said that. Anyway, she had another idea."

"I'll bet she did," Cam said. This sounded exactly like one of Aunt Dixie's schemes.

Prudence continued, "She had another older woman with her and told us she wanted to take my place on the cruise liner. It sounded like such a good idea when she explained it. I could spend time with my family, and she and her friend could enjoy a free luxury vacation. She also mentioned something about fixing Alexandria up with one of her nephews."

"And how did she plan to do all this without being found out?"

Prudence brightened. "Her friend is a shifter. Can you believe it? I wouldn't have, if her friend didn't just change right in front of my eyes. I could swear it was you, Alexandria. And then she shifted into me. It was amazing! She said her friend would pretend to be both you and me, and no one would ever find out."

She looked at Ria with pleading eyes. "I knew you didn't want to even be on this trip with the FitzOsbern boy. My aunt really wanted me to stay and visit, I wanted to stay and visit, so… I agreed."

Cam refused to be diverted. "How did my aunt know that Alexandria wasn't going to go back to the ship?"

"She's *your* aunt?"

"Yes. Now answer the question, please."

"She said she spoke to her and was certain Alexandria planned to stay with her nephew."

Cam looked at Ria. "You talked to my aunt?"

Ria started to shake her head. Then something she'd almost forgotten popped into her head. "Wait. An older woman *did* come by your house. I was half asleep and wasn't going to answer the door, but whoever was ringing the bell was persistent. I thought someone wanted to borrow a cup of sugar."

"A cup of sugar? What morning?"

A beautiful blush filled Ria's cheeks. "The

morning after we met at the karaoke bar. You know, when you left to go to work. It turned out to be an older lady. I thought she was your neighbor."

"What did she say?"

Ria shrugged. "Nothing. She took one look at me, and said never mind."

"What were you wearing?" Cam wondered if she'd answered the door buck naked.

"Um…your shirt."

Prudence blushed until her cheeks were beet red. She cleared her throat. "This young man's aunt was fairly certain you weren't going to make it to the early call back. And I wanted to see Earth and spend time with my aunt and cousins, so I stayed and agreed not to tell anyone." She paused. "I'm sorry about everything."

"What's the return plan?" Cam asked, ignoring all the blushing between the two women.

Prudence said, "I'm supposed to wear a hat and some Earther clothing to disguise myself for the arrival and wait for the ship to dock. When they release everyone, I'm to just slip back on board as though I never left."

"What about Ria?"

Prudence shrugged. "Your aunt said that by the time the ship returned, she expected that Alexandria would want to stay on Earth, but that whatever happened, no one would know that she and I were not on the ten-day trip."

Cam wondered what his aunt was up to. He

hated to get her in trouble when basically she'd done him a huge favor by allowing him to spend the last week with Ria. Whatever happened, his time was running out.

Ria said to Prudence, "You know I don't want to marry Dirt… I mean Douglass, right?"

"Yes, my lady. I did get that impression on the initial trip to Earth. And if I might speak out of turn, Mr. FitzOsbern was not very kind to you."

"Thank you, Prudence. I wish my mother understood what manner of man he is."

"He doesn't let her see it," Prudence said.

"What?"

"He only shows your mother his good side, which in my opinion makes it hard for her to understand why you don't want to have anything to do with him."

"Do you think it would matter?"

"Yes, I do. I don't think she wants you to be unhappy. She believes Mr. FitzOsbern is nicer than he is. He makes sure she sees only his best behavior." Prudence's cheeks flushed again. Cam wondered why, but didn't want to upset her more by pointing it out.

Gage came back in to shoo Cam and Ria out. "She needs to rest."

"Will she be able to get back on the ship and return to Alpha-Prime in two days?" Cam asked.

"I should think so. Her stomach will hurt for several more days, but with the antidote, she shouldn't have any permanent damage. I'll give her some medication for the pain. She'll be fine. They will all be fine, don't worry. We caught it very early."

Cam grabbed Ria's hand and pulled her toward the door.

"Where are you going?" Gage asked.

"If the current danger and drama have been resolved, I'd like to spend the next two days alone with Ria. Tell Axel, Diesel, Jack and anyone else asking about me that I don't want to be disturbed. We'll be on the platform when the ship docks."

Gage smiled. "Will do. Have fun."

Cam didn't respond, but that was exactly what he intended to do. Have fun with Ria until the moment she had to leave. Maybe she could convince her mother to end the arranged marriage, but Cam didn't want to count on that.

He could only count on the next two days to prove that no matter what happened, he loved her and would do anything for her.

Chapter 18

Ria and Cam went back to his house after discovering that the crust-fish fever scare was just that, a scare. Cam texted each of his brothers to repeat what he'd told Prudence and Gage about wanting privacy for the next two days.

They spent the rest of the day and night wrapped in each other's arms, talking about anything that came to mind as their time together brutally ticked down. They ate dinner holding hands and, with the exception of bathroom breaks, didn't stray farther than a few inches from each other over the next twenty-four hours.

Cam kissed her anytime he wanted and she enjoyed every lip-licking moment. They hadn't slept together since the morning after he discovered she was about to be engaged to another guy and that hadn't changed since they left Prudence in the medical area in the basement at the Big Bang Truck Stop.

"Tomorrow around noon, the ship will return," she said, noting they had one last day together.

And one last night.

"Yep."

"I'm going to talk to my mother before she even gets off the ship."

He nodded and smiled, but his eyes didn't look happy.

"I really will."

"And I believe you. I just don't think it will make any difference." He smoothed a palm over her hair, tucking a loose strand behind her ear. "She doesn't like me. Even if the wedding arrangement with Dirt Bag falls through, I'm not the next choice on her list of potential mates for you."

"I only have one name on *my* list."

"Oh?" He acted nonchalant, but she couldn't resist playing.

"That sheriff that looks like an Alpha, what's his name?"

"Wyatt?"

"Oh, yes. Him."

"He's on your list?"

"No. All I'm saying is that he looks like an Alpha, but I know he isn't one because I read his mind."

"I remember," Cam said sourly.

She giggled. "Oh, don't be that way. You know *yours* is the only name on my list of possible marriage candidates."

"It better be. What did you read in the sheriff's

mind besides him liking the blue streaks in your hair?"

"You caught that, huh?" She shrugged. "I don't know. What did you have in mind?"

"Do you know why he was meeting Diesel?"

"No. But he was thinking about another girl when he thought about my hair, namely, how blue streaks would look in *her* hair."

"Oh, yeah? Wyatt has a girlfriend? Interesting. Who is it?"

"I don't know. He started thinking about man things next."

"Man things?"

"You know like motors and vehicle stuff, specifically oil that goes into car engines or something and I stopped listening."

"I wonder why he wanted to talk to Diesel about this girl."

"Don't know."

"I wonder if she's an Alpha and the girl sent him to Diesel to get permission."

"Permission?"

"Well, if an Alpha wants to date a human or get married, there are certain protocols involved."

"Protocols are stupid." Ria hoped the Alpha girl involved with Sheriff Wyatt didn't have to go through the same issues to date and marry the one she loved.

"Why?"

"Protocol is the biggest reason I'm in an arranged marriage."

"If you weren't in an arranged marriage, how would we have ever met?"

"I would have made my way to Earth one of these days."

Cam hugged her close. "What if this is our last night together?" he whispered.

"I will refuse to marry him. He hasn't even proposed. And if he does, I'll say no."

"Can't your mother dictate the acceptance?"

"I'd like to try to see anyone, including my mother, force me."

"I'd pay money and bring the popcorn to see that, but we have to face the possibility we don't want to happen. If your mother finds out that you spent the last ten days here on Earth, she could have me fired, brought up on charges and sent to a gulag."

Ria felt her eyes fill with tears. She did not want Cam to suffer on her account. She was the one who'd defied the rules openly and repeatedly. He only shielded her when it was too late to do anything after the ship had left.

Whatever else she did, Ria would not let Cam be hurt by this adventure—even if she had to endure a lifetime with Dirt Bag FitzOsbern as punishment.

"How do you want to spend what might possibly be your last night here on Earth?" Cam asked.

Ria stared deeply into his eyes. "You know exactly what I want."

"Do I?"

"Yes." She stared at his mouth, lifting her eyes slowly to his desire-filled gaze.

Inhaling deeply, he said softly, "I want that, too."

"What are you saying?" Ria tilted her head to one side.

"I'm saying that my wild, roguish nature just punched my honorable intent in the face and it went down without a whimper."

"Go, wild, roguish side." Ria leaned forward and kissed him hard on the mouth.

Cam held her, tightened his arms around her and kissed her back like…well, like a wild rogue finally let loose to do what he wanted.

Ria broke the luscious kiss. "Wait. I have an idea."

Cam took a deep breath. "Idea?" he asked, sounding like he didn't quite understand the word.

"Please, could we go to your property?"

"Tonight?"

"Yes. Please. Then when we wake up tomorrow, the view will be so lovely and perfect." She grinned, feeling the heat come into her cheeks. They hadn't slept together since karaoke night. She wanted one chance to wake up, with him, to the beautiful lake view. One last, flawless memory, just in case things didn't go the way she planned when she informed her mother she wouldn't marry Dirt Bag.

"For the record, from my perspective the view is always lovely when I wake up next to you. But if you truly want to sleep at the cabin tonight—"

"I really do." Ria kissed his face over and over.

"—then your wish is my command."

Cam quickly packed a bag. Ria picked up her faithful travel knapsack, the one she'd smuggled off the ship before sneaking away from the truck stop's basement facility. It held the precious intelligence she'd obtained about the bus stop on the highway near the way station, the Earther dollars needed to ride it and the information that there was a karaoke bar in nearby Old Coot. She'd never have gotten away without it. The original plan had been to catch a bus right after the bar closed and be back in Alienn by two in the morning. Instead, she'd gone home with Cam.

Best decision ever.

Cam slung his bag over his shoulder. Ria slipped both arms into the knapsack straps and lifted it onto her back.

"Want to take the motorcycle?" Cam asked.

"Of course."

Cam was her best decision ever.

The steady roar of an outboard motor crossing the lake woke Cam from likely the best sleep he'd had in his life. He felt the warm body snuggled against his side. He opened his eyes and saw a thick strand of blue-streaked hair. He inhaled deeply and a familiar perfume filled his lungs. Ria, soft and warm, was wrapped around him like his favorite blanket. Her long dark hair—with the streaks of blue—splayed over his chest and her arm cocooned them.

If he could stay right here forever, just like this, he'd consider himself a lucky man.

Morning sunlight poured in from the window and lit the cabin wall. Ria had insisted they leave the curtains wide open before they fell asleep. She wanted to see the lake first thing when she woke up. Cam wanted to see *her* first thing when he woke up.

Mission accomplished.

Unfortunately, with the morning also came the cold, hard reality that he and Ria only had a few hours left together. He glanced at the battery-operated clock on the nightstand, noting the alarm he'd set would go off in half an hour.

That meant just three and a half hours before the ship docked. After that, their future together was uncertain. He breathed deeply, gathering her lovely scent into his lungs, wanting to memorize every second of the rest of their limited time together.

Last night had been even more amazing than their first night together, which—make no mistake—had been pretty spectacular. How would he ever live without her?

The worst-case scenario plan slid into his head and he spent a few moments thinking about how he might fake her death, hide her at the cabin and claim ignorance as to her whereabouts. His brothers would take one look at him and know exactly what he was doing. They would probably all lie for him, but when they got caught—and they would—they'd *all* get into serious trouble. He couldn't have that.

Ria stirred, breaking up the vision of his unwise daydream. He watched her, wanting to see her wake up and realize where she was.

She lifted her head up from his shoulder, but her eyes remained closed. She couldn't be more adorable if she tried. Slowly, one eye opened halfway, and then the other. She turned her head toward the light and both eyes opened wide. She sucked in a deep breath. "Oh, the view," she breathed, her voice husky with sleep and sexy as hell. Awe and delight wreathed her face. So beautiful.

"The lake. The tall trees. Stunning. I love it." She turned to him and pointed out the window. "Did you see?"

Cam kept his gaze on her. "I did, but you are much more beautiful." He tucked a strand of loose hair behind one ear.

She cocked her head. "What's that noise?"

"Just a boat motor."

She turned to stare at him. He was grinning.

"What's so funny?"

"Nothing. I just love watching you wake up to see the lake view."

"It's more beautiful than I imagined." She sighed. "Thank you for bringing me here."

"My pleasure." Oh, yes. There had been a lot of pleasure last night and into this morning.

She grinned back before asking, "How much time do we have?"

"Plenty."

"Time enough to sit outside and watch the water before we leave?"

"Of course."

Ten minutes later, they were dressed. He took her hand and they walked to the lake's edge by way of the dock.

She sat cross-legged on the wooden boards and he sat beside her. "After you look your fill at the lake, I thought we'd go back to my house in town. We can shower and have a nice breakfast before..." He didn't bother finishing the sentence. They both knew what happened next.

"Okay."

Out on the lake, the boat that had woken him curved around and headed back in their direction. Cam could see fishing equipment and a cooler aboard between an older couple. He and Ria both waved. The couple waved back. All around them, birds tweeted and called to each other, and the wind rustled the leaves in the trees as the scent of wildflowers filled the air. Cam kissed Ria, taking in all the details he could in this perfect place while they shared it one last time.

It couldn't be put off any longer. They returned to the cabin. Silently, as though following a long-established routine, they tidied up. Too soon, they were back on the bike, headed away from the lake property.

There was no wild revving of the bike's engine, no racing along the highway at speeds that made Ria squeal and laugh and hold him tight. Cam drove the bike slowly back to his house so they could get ready for the inevitable.

Once inside, Ria behaved like this wasn't the last they'd ever see of each other. They made breakfast together. While she stirred the beaten chicken eggs in a flat pan, Cam made the toast and bacon. She was a quick study. They ate in companionable silence, staring at each other, lingering over the last of their coffee.

They cleaned everything up and then he couldn't resist taking her in his arms, and just holding her. She burrowed against his chest like she belonged there.

Finally, when their time was up—and not a second sooner—Cam and Ria entered the basement facility in time to see the *Royal Caldera Forte* docking. The posted schedule noted the ship would depart tomorrow at midnight. A day and a half left.

Cam squeezed her hand. She grinned, the look on her face full of confidence. He wasn't foolish enough to expect her mother to change her mind, but smiled anyway because she was so beautiful.

Director Patmore led the way as passengers poured from of all three of the ship's exits. He looked at Ria as though surprised to see her.

Ria kissed Cam goodbye.

"I'll meet you right here in one hour," she whispered. "I promise. I *know* I can convince my mother to stop this stupid arranged marriage."

Cam nodded and watched until she was out of sight.

Sighing, feeling at a loss, he looked around the lounge and spotted Axel. He shoved his hands in his pockets and headed in his brother's direction. He might as well sit in while Director Patmore gave his report. It was either that or run crazed through the ship's corridors, screaming Ria's name.

Axel looked relieved to see him, then his face fell. When Cam got close enough, he asked, "Where is…you know?"

He glanced at Director Patmore, who had almost reached them.

"She went to have a talk with her mother."

"Hello, gentlemen. Good to see you both." Director Patmore seemed downright jovial.

"How was your trip? Any problems with the volcanic ash along the route?" Axel queried.

Director Patmore glanced at his electronic

clipboard briefly and then said, "Excellent. No problems at all, I'm happy to report."

"Good."

The ship's director read the highlights of the ten-day trip from his electronic clipboard while Cam and Axel tried to look interested.

"Sounds like a great trip." Cam thought Axel did a good job of pretending to sound enthused. The best Cam could manage was not looking hostile, and he was certain his feelings came through anyway. Today was no different. Thankfully, Axel kept working his professional magic with the client. "We'll get you fueled and ready for your departure. In the meantime, we hope your crew and passengers can enjoy the way station."

Axel started to move away, but stopped when Patmore made a face.

"Problem?" Axel narrowed his eyes as if daring Patmore to speak.

Patmore looked at his clipboard. "Oh, I'm sorry. Apparently you weren't notified."

"Notified?" Axel asked.

"Yes. Our travel plans changed en route."

"En route?" Axel echoed, shooting Cam a surprised look.

"The *Royal Caldera Forte* will be departing at midnight tonight, not tomorrow. And if we can leave sooner, that would be best. The passengers have been told to return to the ship no later than eight o'clock."

"Why the change?" Cam asked.

The director glanced back at the ship as if to assure himself no one important was listening in. "One of our very important guests has made an emergency request to return as soon as possible to Alpha-Prime."

"Who?" Cam suspected Ria's mother had raised a fuss. She'd somehow found out about him and Ria and wanted to get home as fast as possible before her golden goose escaped.

Patmore looked aghast. "I'm sorry, but I'm not at liberty to share *that* information, gentlemen. Suffice it to say that the request came from a very important guest. As always, the Royal Caldera Cruise Line wants to accommodate our special guests. We shall be leaving in just under twelve hours or sooner, if you can arrange it. Thank you, gentlemen."

Cam tried not to let his anger at losing precious time with Ria boil over, but knew he'd failed when his brother stared at his clenched fists.

Axel said hurriedly, "We'll do what we can, Director Patmore, but we may not be able to refuel you until tomorrow morning. We are awaiting a fuel shipment later tonight." Axel looked down as if bummed about this complication. "If only you had notified us earlier, we might have been able to accommodate you."

Patmore looked at Axel and then at Cam. "I see." He examined his clipboard, as if it would give him the proper response. "Well, please do what you can. Perhaps you can expedite the fuel order."

Axel nodded. "It was already expedited to be on hand to refuel the cruise liner for departure tomorrow night, but I'll see what we can do. How'd that be?"

Patmore gave a curt nod. "I'd be grateful." He eyed Cam narrowly, as though this might be his fault, then turned on his heel and marched back toward the ship, possibly to tell his "very important guest" that the ship wouldn't be able to leave early.

Cam leaned toward Axel once Patmore was out of earshot. "Are you really waiting on a fuel shipment?"

"What do you think?"

"Thanks, Bro." A reprieve, if only a small one. He'd take it.

They looked up to see Ria exit the Elite door, marching in a straight line toward them both. The fire in her eyes told him things hadn't gone well with her mother.

"You don't have to tell me," Cam said as she got close. "Your mother doesn't want to call off the arranged marriage."

Ria inhaled deeply and exhaled her ire. "That is correct."

"Did she realize you'd been gone and off the ship for the last ten days?"

She smiled. "Nope. That's the only good news."

Axel said, "Did she say she asked for the return flight to be tonight instead of tomorrow?"

Ria frowned. "No. Why? Is the ship leaving tonight?" She looked at Cam and her eyes glistened with tears.

Cam nodded. "My brother here told Director Patmore that we have a fuel shortage and won't be able to refuel until tomorrow."

"Thanks, Axel." Ria hugged him around his neck.

He patted her on the back and gave Cam a sheepish look. "You two go have fun while I see if I can delay the fuel shipment as long as possible."

Cam led Ria to a coffee shop in the way station. They sat across from each other, sipped coffee and stared into each other's eyes for quite a long time without saying anything.

After a lengthy quiet, Cam broke the silence, wanting to hear her voice. It was probably sappy, but at this point he didn't care. "What else did you tell your mother?"

Ria shrugged. "I told her that I didn't like Douglass. I don't want to marry him and if she forced me I'd be miserable for the rest of my life."

"And she said?"

"She seemed surprised."

"Why?"

"I guess she thought that I'd been sneaking out to see him all through the whole trip and that we were getting along well. I can't imagine why. Your aunt and her friend were obviously not going out to see Dirt Bag."

"Knowing my aunt, she was probably out gambling. She calls that her guilty pleasure for entertainment. Either that, or she gets up on her high horse and labels it a possible chance to earn free money for the old folks' home in town." Cam straightened. "Did you happen to see my aunt or her friend aboard or near your room?"

"Nope. I stopped by my suite on my way to see my mother, but the place looks exactly like I left it."

"Maybe we should find my aunt Dixie and discover what she did on the trip."

"Obviously, she did a good job of being me, because my mother was completely fooled."

"What did your mother say about your hair?"

Ria laughed. "Oh! Shockingly, she wasn't a fan."

"That *is* shocking."

"I believe her exact words were, 'Good heavens, Alexandria, what have you done to yourself?' And then she gave me her typical disapproving-parent look."

Out of the corner of his eye, Cam spotted someone moving toward them at a fast clip. He turned as a well-dressed, obviously very wealthy young man approached.

"Alexandria," the man said. "There you are! Where have you been?"

Ria paled and stood up. Cam stood with her.

The man reached into his pocket and pulled out a small box as he came to a stop at their table. *What is he doing?*

He looked into Ria's face, dropped to one knee, held up the box and popped it open to display a huge diamond ring. "Alexandria Latham Borne, will you marry me?"

Chapter 19

Ria wasn't often at a complete loss for words, but having Dirt Bag FitzOsbern drop to one knee and propose in front of the love of her life rendered her absolutely speechless.

Her mouth opened. Nothing came out. She closed her mouth. She tried again. Open. Nothing.

"Alexandria?" Dirt Bag prodded, looking at Cam with annoyance. "Well, will you?"

Why is he doing this? What is he up to?

He didn't want to marry her before. She recalled easily the lip curl he'd exhibited the last time the topic came up. Her mother had, of course, been the only one talking about their marriage and how wonderful it would be.

Dirt Bag huffed impatiently. "Are you going to answer me?"

"No. I will *not* marry you."

"What? Why not?" Dirt Bag stood up, looking clueless as to why she didn't fall to the ground at his feet and accept his unexpected proposal after snubbing her for the entire trip from Alpha-Prime to Earth.

Oh no. A horrible thought occurred to her. What had happened with Cam's aunt on the trip? Had she done something to make Dirt Bag want to marry Ria? That didn't seem likely, given what Prudence had said. It sounded like Cam's aunt wanted Ria with her nephew. She wouldn't want Dirt Bag to propose. Would she?

Operating on instinct alone, Ria asked, "Do you happen to remember the journey to Earth the first time? You couldn't be bothered to speak to me the whole trip." Maybe he'd give her a clue. Hopefully, the imposter taking her place hadn't done anything to change his mind about their future together. "So, tell me what has changed in the last ten days, huh? What?"

Dirt Bag tilted his head so far back she thought it might fall right off his shoulders. He snapped it forward. "I know we didn't see much of each other on this trip, but that will change now."

"Will it?"

"Sure. Now I *want* to spent time with you."

Cam looked like he was about to tear Dirt Bag limb from limb. She had to get to the bottom of this. Fast. "Why?"

"Why else? You'll be my wife." He shrugged. "And once we get married, you can talk all you want."

In an imperious way that only a FitzOsbern could pull off, Dirt Bag looked around the way station, his expression eloquent in his disappointment at the array and variety of shops and eating places. Were they not up to his exacting standards?

Ria leaned against Cam's side, gathering strength. "What if *I* don't want to talk to *you*?"

"Fine. Whatever. Don't talk. That's up to you." He kept searching the area as if not finding what he was looking for.

"So, is there a place we can get married here on Earth somewhere?" he asked a bit distracted.

"What!"

His gaze returned to her from the fruitless search. "I thought we should get married right away. We can go back to Alpha-Prime already married and then have a big party with my parents. What do you think?"

"I think you're...off your rocker." *The Earther phrase book comes in handy once again.*

Dirt Bag frowned. "What does that mean?"

"It means she thinks you're crazy," Cam said. "So do I, by the way."

Dirt Bag stood up and eyed Cam. "Who in the deep dark space potato patch are you?"

"Don't use that language with me." Hostility came off Cam in waves. Ria wanted to wrap herself around him, but it probably wouldn't be appropriate. She slid in front of Cam so he wouldn't give in to the temptation to punch the pompous idiot. The FitzOsberns, as a rule, didn't forgive bad behavior and had been known to prosecute folks for less.

Dirt Bag turned his fierce gaze from Cam and focused on her. "I thought you were hot to marry me for my money." He looked even more pretentious than he usually did. "So let's go get married. What's the issue?"

"Listen closely, because I'm only going to say this one more time. I will *never* marry you."

Dirt Bag frowned. His mouth opened like he was about to offer up a threat, but his gaze went over her shoulder and he relaxed. "We'll just see about that, won't we?"

Ria turned to see her mother on a fast march toward the three of them.

Oh no. Her mother would probably accept his proposal for Ria on the spot and insist they elope as soon as possible. She might also produce a clergyman and a shotgun to ensure the bride agreed to this horrible, awful, pending arranged marriage in a timely fashion.

Doom cavorted within her soul, doing a hateful dance of glee.

Cam wanted to pick up Ria and run when her odious intended dropped to one knee and proposed. At first FitzOsbern had seemed sincere, whipping out a gargantuan diamond ring—the kind Cam could *never* afford to give her.

But as the conversation went on, it became clear

the other man had something else on his mind. FitzOsbern didn't seem to want to marry Ria. It was more like he *needed* to marry her. Cam wondered what the guy was up to. It was obvious Ria thought the same thing, but she looked over her shoulder and seemed to deflate. Cam followed her gaze and saw why her spirit seemed to sag and why FitzOsbern seemed so smug all of a sudden.

Governess Ruth Latham Borne marched toward them like a battalion chief about to go into combat. She moved at a fast clip, staring down the three of them like lasers would shoot out of her eyes at any moment, target Cam especially and burn him to the ground until only a pile of ash remained.

"What is going on here?"

FitzOsbern puffed up, showed her the ring box and said, "I've just asked your daughter to marry me, twice. She's turned me down, twice." Ria's mother turned on her daughter as FitzOsbern continued, "Now that you're here, perhaps you can talk some sense into her."

"Alexandria," Governess Latham Borne said between gritted teeth. "Do you wish to marry this man or not?"

Ria straightened "I told you before, Mother. My answer is no." A tear slipped down her cheek. "I will never marry Douglass Barnard FitzOsbern willingly."

Governess Latham Borne turned to FitzOsbern, cleared her throat and said, "Well, young man, you have your answer. My daughter does not wish to marry you."

FitzOsbern stood stunned, mouth opening and closing like a crust-fish's. He wasn't alone in his shock. Ria exchanged a look with Cam, who was also flabbergasted. He lifted a shoulder in puzzlement. Ria's mother looked rather...satisfied, for lack of a better word.

FitzOsbern found his voice. "I beg your pardon, madam?"

"I doubt that very much. You've been quite a nasty little crust-fish on this whole trip and well before we ever boarded the *Royal Caldera Forte* on Alpha-Prime. But let me tell you something, your antics have not gone unnoticed."

"My antics? Little crust-fish? Are you out of your head, woman?" FitzOsbern's tone was the epitome of disbelief.

"No. I believe I understand things quite clearly, maybe for the first time since I've known you."

Cam noticed two women approaching, one obviously pregnant, the other holding a baby.

FitzOsbern saw the women and his face went white and waxy. He thrust the ring box in Ria's hand and grabbed her upper arms. Cam clamped his hands around the man's wrists to force him to let go, but he held fast.

"Alexandria, you *must* marry me. Today! Our union has been arranged since you were a child. We were meant to be together."

"Let go of her or I'll break both of your arms," Cam gritted out.

FitzOsbern must have realized he meant it and let go. Ria stepped back. Cam let go of the other man and wrapped his arms around her, resting his chin on her shoulder, claiming her for all the world to see and doing his best to ensure the man knew she was off-limits.

The pregnant woman called out, "We need to talk to you, Fitz."

The baby let out a wail loud enough to reach the outer atmosphere. FitzOsbern looked like he'd tasted something sour.

"Aren't you going to go comfort your child, *Fitz*?" Governess Latham Borne asked.

"I beg your pardon. I do not know these base women."

"That's very interesting. You certainly seemed to know them well enough back on board the ship."

FitzOsbern shook his head. "Not true. Never seen them before."

Governess Latham Borne straightened her spine. "I am a witness."

"Witness to what?"

"I am a witness to you admitting that you are the father of Lissa's baby girl and that you also are the father of MaryAnn's unborn child. You promised them both you would take care of them once you got back to Alpha-Prime. You said you would marry them. I heard you."

"I never said that," FitzOsbern insisted. His tone turned even nastier. "Besides, if your daughter and I don't marry, you won't get the bride payment promised in the arranged marriage papers."

"You're a liar. You did tell each of those two young women separately you'd marry them," the Governess said. "I would not allow you to marry my daughter for all the credits in this galaxy or the next. And I will ensure your parents know exactly why. As a matter of fact, I intend to make sure all of Alpha-Prime's elite know exactly what sort of immoral, cowardly man you are."

Director Patmore approached, communication video screen in one hand and his ever-present electronic clipboard in the other. He seemed oblivious to the growing audience as he said, "Oh, Mr. FitzOsbern, I've been looking for you. Two things. First, unfortunately, we won't be able to leave tonight."

"Why not?" FitzOsbern drew himself up to his full height—still several inches shorter than Cam's. He was kind of a runty Alpha.

"Apparently, the ship's fuel won't be delivered until tomorrow afternoon."

"Space potatoes!"

"Why are you in such an all-fired hurry to leave?" Governess Latham Borne asked. "Do you have more unwed mothers on the way from all parts of the galaxy, looking for you to make good on your fake promises to marry them?"

Director Patmore looked like he might swallow his clipboard. "Oh…uhm…and two, Mr. FitzOsbern, your parents wish to speak with you." He held out the communication video screen.

"What?!" If FitzOsbern had looked pale before, he now looked colorless as Director Patmore pushed a button and the images of an older couple appeared on the screen.

"Douglass," the woman said. "We have received some rather disturbing information while you've been gone."

"Mother," FitzOsbern said. "I'm busy right now. I can't really talk—"

"Don't get sassy with your mother," the male half of the couple said.

Governess Latham Borne leaned close to the screen. "Your son is a disgrace and should be neutered as soon as possible."

Their mouths fell open. "What are you saying?" the man asked.

"I don't know exactly how many grandchildren you already have, however, you should likely expect more. There's one adorable little girl here, and a young woman is carrying another child. Beyond that, who knows how many grandchildren you may meet in the next few months from seemingly all corners of the galaxies we visited on this trip?

"In light of this, I cordially withdraw from our agreement to join our children in matrimony on the grounds of blatant and egregious pre-marital infidelity and persistent and appalling bad judgment. To that end, I intend to submit testimony and evidence outlining that your son has fathered at least four children, and that there are at a minimum two more children on the way. I refuse to put my only daughter into that volatile, emotional and financially draining set of circumstances. No decent mother would.

"Good day, sir and madam."

The senior Mr. FitzOsbern started to speak, but Ria's mother cut him off. "I said, good day, sir." She stepped away from the video screen.

The young woman with the baby stepped close and held the child up to the screen. "This is your granddaughter. I named her Beatrice." The baby wailed apparently unimpressed with meeting her grandparents for the first time.

Governess Latham Borne eyed the way Cam had his arms wrapped around Ria.

"I see you found my daughter."

"I did."

"Is *he* the reason you don't want to marry the FitzOsbern boy?"

"No. I never wanted to marry Douglass," Ria said quietly. Cam was so used to her calling him Dirt Bag that he almost asked who Douglass was. "But I'm in love with this man. And I want a future with him."

Cam expected the Governess to snatch her

daughter away. He unconsciously tightened his grip on Ria.

"I'm not certain that's what is in your best interest, Alexandria, but we can discuss it at length at a later time."

"What are you going to do, Mother?"

"I must get our belongings off the ship before it departs. Prudence is already packing up as we speak. She's delighted for the opportunity to visit her family, of course. However, we are all stranded here on the Earth colony now."

"We are?"

"This trip was bought and paid for by the FitzOsberns. I don't expect they will want to fund our return journey to Alpha-Prime now that I've spoken my mind."

"For which I'm very grateful."

Her mother sniffed and looked uncomfortable. "I'm only after your best interests, Alexandria."

"I know."

Cam wasn't quite ready to celebrate. The shocking turn of events made a future with Ria more than possible, but not guaranteed. He expected her mother would have a say in whether he remained in her life. He couldn't imagine the Governess would want to remain on a colony planet for very long. The moment she secured funds to return to Alpha-Prime, she'd likely kidnap Ria and head back pronto.

From behind him, a familiar voice piped up, "Hey, Cam, did you miss me?"

He turned and stared down at Aunt Dixie and her cohort in crime, Miss Penny.

"I suspect you know I was pretty busy away from the truck stop and the way station," he said.

The elderly woman beamed. "Well, I figured that. At least I hoped so, anyway."

For the first time in recent memory, Cam relaxed as he faced a conversation with his wacky and unpredictable aunt. "Did *you* have a good trip?" Given her jubilant expression, he suspected she had.

"It was dandy. Those luxury cruise lines sure know how to treat their guests."

Aunt Dixie saw Ria's mother watching and waggled her fingers in a wave. "Well, hello there. How are you?"

The Governess's eyes narrowed suspiciously. "I'm sorry. Have we met?"

Miss Penny leaned in and whispered something in Aunt Dixie's ear. "Right. I forgot." She stuck out her hand. "My name is Dixie Lou Grey. This here is my best friend, Miss Penny."

"Charmed to meet you," the Governess said, looking only slightly uncomfortable.

"Say, have you ever considered living on Earth?"

Ria's mother managed to look only slightly horrified. "Earth?"

"Let me tell you about the old folks' home here in Alienn. It's the best place to live for us girls getting up in years. You know what I mean, honey." Aunt Dixie poked Ria's mother in the ribs. "Say, you look pretty good, though." Aunt Dixie studied her face carefully, as though inspecting it for flaws. "Have you had some work done?"

"Work? Done?" Ria's mother sounded genuinely puzzled.

"You know, like a little nip and tuck, a bit of plastic surgery." Aunt Dixie squinted at her hairline. "Whoever your doctor is, he's marvelous."

"I beg your pardon."

"Oh, no worries, you're excused." Aunt Dixie looped her arm through Ruth Latham Borne's and pulled her away from Cam and Ria. "Say, how do you feel about fundraisers?"

Ria put a hand over her mouth as a giggle escaped.

"What's so funny?" Cam asked.

"I love your aunt Dixie. It definitely was her who came to your door that morning after the night at the karaoke bar. I can totally believe she talked Prudence into going along with her plan to swap places."

"She's the wiliest woman I know." The emotion Cam usually associated with Aunt Dixie was irritation, closely followed by exasperation. Now, he felt only pride and gratitude. His aunt had done him a huge favor. He'd have to return the gesture with a huge IOU. He only hoped he wouldn't end up buck naked in a calendar to benefit the old folks' home.

"Do you think she could talk my mother into staying here?"

"Are you kidding? She could sell overpriced sand to a desert dweller."

Ria laughed. "Well, I'm grateful to her."

"Truth is, so am I."

"What happens now?"

Cam pulled a modest engagement ring from his pocket. He'd kept it in his pocket these last few days, hoping it would serve as a talisman to bring them luck as their time together wound down. He didn't have a fancy box. The diamond wasn't the size of a golf ball, like the one Dirt Bag had offered her. But the ring had special meaning to him. It had been passed down in the Grey family. It wasn't extravagant or gigantic, but he wanted Ria to have it.

"I wondered if you would marry me."

Ria's hands went to her face. She sucked in a deep breath of surprise. She stared at the ring like it was a life preserver and she was drowning. She reached for it slowly, as if it would be snatched away if she grabbed for it too quickly.

"Now that you seem to be free from your previous obligation, I want to ensure you understand my feelings. I love you. I want you to be my wife. I want to wake up every single day like we did this morning. Please say you'll marry me, Ria. I promise to do everything in my power to make you happy."

"I would love to marry you." Ria held her hand out so Cam could slide the ring on her finger.

"Do you want to get married today?"

"*Can* we get married today?"

"Sure. We *are* a full-service way station. We *do* have a Justice of the Peace on call and at the ready for couples arriving on ships, wanting an official Earther-style wedding upon their arrival."

Ria looked like he had just handed her the moon. "I love you so much. I want to marry you as soon as possible."

"I love you, too. Let's go."

"Should we tell anyone?"

Cam shrugged. "We can. Or we can tell them afterward."

Ria nodded. "Yes. Afterward is a great idea."

Epilogue

Two months later, the lakeside cabin

Ria was so happy, she could have skipped to the bedroom. Common sense, and the two cups of hot coffee she carried, kept her steps even. So she grinned ear to ear with joy and thought about skipping down to the dock later.

In the bedroom, she paused to gaze at the breathtaking view out the window of her new home. "Have I ever told you how much I love the view from right here?" Ria asked, handing Cam his morning coffee.

"Once or twice," he said with a grin. "I'm glad you still enjoy it."

She seated herself at the little table they'd put on the deck outside their bedroom.

"I will never get tired of it, husband of mine." Ria leaned close to get a coffee-flavored kiss. She loved saying "husband" and thinking it and, most especially, living it.

"What shall we do today, wife of mine?"

"I have to go into town for a meeting."

"A meeting?"

"Didn't I tell you? Juliana and I have formed a two-person group called the Grey Brothers Wives' Club."

Cam laughed. "So you just have the two members so far, then."

"Right, but eventually I'm certain there will be more."

"So if Valene ever gets married, will her future husband be allowed to join this club?"

"Of course. Juliana and I have already discussed it. He will be our very special, one and only male member." She giggled uproariously at her play on words. "Get it?"

Cam shook his head. "Got it."

Ria sipped her favorite pumpkin spice coffee and moaned in delight at both the taste of her beverage, the view of the lake surrounded by tall trees and her perfect life that she never expected to have. She was so very grateful.

"How is your mother?"

"She's settling in better than I ever expected. She spends most of her time with your aunt Dixie and Miss Penny. I heard Diesel call them the Treacherous Trinity the other day."

Cam smiled. "Good one, and likely accurate, too."

"What are you going to do today while I'm in town with Juliana?"

"I have a bunch of rowdy guys coming over for a big party."

"Really?"

He reached over to playfully tweak her nose. "No. I hired a group of workmen to come in and finish the bathrooms and the kitchen. We will have a fully functional home by the end of the day."

"Awesome. Maybe we *should* throw a rowdy party."

"Oh? Is that on your revised list of things to do here on Earth?"

"Not yet. But I can certainly add it."

"Good idea, wife of mine."

Ria leaned back in her chair, mug cupped in her hands. The wind off the lake ruffled Cam's hair on his brow, much the same way she enjoyed ruffling his hair. The surface of the water was glass smooth, forming a perfect mirror of shore, trees and sky. Somewhere on the lake, a jumping fish splashed, and a loon called to its mate.

Cam caught her watching him. His lips curled in that sexy smile that had drawn her to him at the karaoke bar. Once she'd seen it, she thought she'd follow him anywhere. Now, she knew it.

"What time are the workmen coming?"

"Oh, not for a while."

She put her mug down and stood. "Good." At the slider, she cast a glance over her shoulder. "Coming?"

His mug hit the table with a thunk, coffee sloshed over the rim, and she ran for the bed, leading him right where she wanted him.

The End.

Available Now

YOU'VE GOT ALIENS

Alienn, Arkansas 1

Librarian and aspiring journalist Juliana Masters has a mystery to solve: Who am I? Armed with the truth about her past, she can leave her humdrum present behind and get on with her future. She just needs to complete one lucrative investigative writing assignment and she'll be on her way. All she has to do is prove aliens live and work out of a secret facility based under the Big Bang Truck Stop. No problem. Getting her socks knocked off by the Fearless Leader isn't part of the plan.

Diesel Grey worked for years to achieve his goal of heading up the family business in Alienn, Arkansas. Mission accomplished, but being Fearless Leader of a galactic way station comes with a lot more headaches than anticipated. It's hard to consider the shockingly well-informed writer a headache, though, especially when she makes him ache in all the right places.

If he's not careful, he'll give her everything she needs to blow his family's cover and expose to the human world that aliens do walk among them.

All he really wants to do is sweep her up in his arms and never let her go.

Available Now

ALIENS ACTUALLY

A Nocturne Falls Universe Collection

Pilot. Guard. Prisoner... *Stowaway.*

All are crashed in the Georgia woods, lost on a world where aliens are the stuff of science fiction. And what if the locals are far from human themselves?

Close Encounters of the Alien Kind

Stella Grey's mission was simple: Locate the downed ship in the Georgia woods. Secure the prisoner. And keep the earthlings from learning that aliens live among them, namely in Alienn, Arkansas.

Prisoner, Draeken Phoenix, is also the dangerously delicious man she left behind on Alpha-Prime to start a new life on Earth.

Invasion of the Alien Snatchers

Riker Phoenix, the guard, has everything but the tantalizing woman who changed the course of his life.

Elise Midori ran a galaxy away to escape the man she loved, but could never have. But it wasn't far enough, thanks to a crash in Nocturne Falls, and a crazy Druid high priestess intent on claiming him as her own.

The Alien Who Fell to Earth

Pilot, Holden Grigori is lost on an alien world, with no memory. A pretty woman claims she's his wife and loves him. He'd do anything for her.

Victoria Greene is sent to find the pilot and keep him safe as he recovers. Pretending to be his wife is not a hardship. Falling in love is even easier. But what happens when he gets his memories back and realizes that to him she is…no one.

Available Now

BIKER

BAD BOYS IN BIG TROUBLE 1

Despite the danger, there are some definite pluses to undercover agent Zak Langston's current alias as a mechanic slash low-life criminal. He doesn't have to shave regularly or keep his hair military short. He gets to ride a damn fine Harley. And then there's the sweet, sexy lady next door who likes to sneak peeks at his butt. Yeah, that was a major plus.

Kaitlin Price has had the worst luck with men. As if her unearned reputation as a frigid tease isn't enough, she also has to deal with her stepsister's casual cruelty and taunting tales of sexual conquests she can only dream of. So Kaitlin has never been with a man. So what? So what…

So maybe the sexy bad boy next door would be willing to help her with that.

Gunfire, gangsters and a kidnapping weren't part of her Deflower Kaitlin plan. Good thing for her bad boy Zak is very, very good. At everything.

Available Now

BOUNCER

BAD BOYS IN BIG TROUBLE 2

DEA Agent Reece Langston has spent a year at the city's hottest club, working his way closer to the core of a money laundering operation. Women throw themselves at him all the time, but there's only one he's interested in catching. And she won't even tell him her name.

FBI Agent Jessica Hayes doesn't know much about the sexy stranger except that he's tall, dark and gorgeous. Best of all, he seems just as drawn to her as she is to him—in other words, he's the perfect man to show one kick-ass virgin what sex is all about. No names, no strings and no regrets.

Their one-night stand turns into two. Then a date. Then…maybe more.

Everything is going deliciously well until Jessica's boss orders her to use her lover to further an FBI operation.

Everything is going deliciously well until Reece's handler orders him to use his lover to get closer to his target.

Is their desire enough to match the danger and deception?

AVAILABLE NOW

BODYGUARD

BAD BOYS IN BIG TROUBLE 3

The baseball stadium is torture for Chloe Wakefield, from the noisy stands to the slimy man her colleague set her up with.

Too bad she isn't with the sexy stud seated on her other side. He shares his popcorn. Shields her from the crowd. And, when the kiss cam swings their way, gives her a lip-lock that knocks her socks into the next county.

Goodbye, vile blind date. Hello, gorgeous stranger.

Staying under the radar is pretty much a job requisite for bodyguard Deke Langston, but he can't resist tasting Chloe's sweet lips. Nor her sweet invitation into her bed, where the sensuous little virgin proceeds to blow his mind.

But someone doesn't like how close they are getting. The thought that scares Deke the most is that another woman in his care might be hurt because of his past.

All of Deke's skills are put to the test as he and Chloe race to solve the puzzle of who is plotting against them.

Chloe's in danger and Deke has never had a more precious body to guard.

AVAILABLE NOW

BOMB TECH

BAD BOYS IN BIG TROUBLE 4

Bomb tech and firefighter Alex Langston has a reputation around the station as a bad-boy, love 'em and leave 'em type, but that couldn't be further from the truth. He wants nothing more than a quiet life after a military tour that saw him in some very hot situations overseas. He garners more than his fair share of feminine attention, but hasn't felt so much as a spark of interest for any woman since landing in Ironwood, Arizona...until now.

Schoolteacher Veronica Quentin was warned to keep her guard up around Alex. The last thing she wants is to be a notch on some sexy stud's bedpost. She's been used before, and knows well the heartache that can bring. But that was before she saw him. And before he rescued her from a mysterious kidnapping that saw her chained half-naked in the town square with a bomb strapped to her chest.

But is Veronica the real target? Or has someone set their sights on Alex?

Until they find out, they can't trust anyone but each other. And the sensual flames that ignite whenever they're together.

AVAILABLE NOW

BOUNTY HUNTER

BAD BOYS IN BIG TROUBLE 5

Dalton Langston has a sixth sense when it comes to tracking his quarry. He has a talent for getting in his prey's mind. Now, the only thing he's interested in hunting is some rest and relaxation in Las Vegas. The last thing he wants is to get dragged into chasing after some runaway rich girl.

Lina Dragovic has eluded everyone her parents have sent after her in their efforts to force her into an arranged marriage. She's served her time as the Dragovic crime family's cloistered daughter. Now all she wants is her freedom. What better place to hide than Sin City, where the bright lights offer the deepest shadows?

But there's no outrunning the dangerously sexy bounty hunter…especially when getting caught by him is so tempting. And so deliciously rewarding.

Falling in love was never part of the plan.

AVAILABLE NOW

BANDIT

BAD BOYS IN BIG TROUBLE 6

Miles Turner, a handler and operative with The Organization, a private security firm, is used to always being the man with the plan, the guy in control of everything around him. He can't imagine any situation that would get the better of him—until he meets Sophie.

Travelling sales rep Sophie Rayburn has been burned by love before, but she's determined not to spend Christmas Eve alone. When she spots sexy Miles at a run-down bar in a Podunk New Mexico bar, she decides he'd make the perfect gift to herself. Why shouldn't she indulge them both with a little holiday cheer between the sheets?

Sensual sparks fly as soon as they come together, like they were made for each other, in bed and out. A kidnapping, a drug scam and a dangerous mole don't stand a chance.

Sweet, sexy Sophie is enough to make even a good man lose total control. And Miles is not good. He's all bad boy.

About the Author

Fiona Roarke is a multi-published author who lives a quiet life with the exception of the characters and stories roaming around in her head. She writes about sexy alpha heroes, using them to launch her first series, Bad Boys in Big Trouble. Next up, a new sci-fi contemporary romance series. When she's not curled on the sofa reading a great book or at the movie theater watching the latest action film, Fiona spends her time writing about the next bad boy (or bad boy alien) who needs his story told.

Want to know when Fiona's next book will be available? Sign up for her Newsletter:
http://eepurl.com/bONukX

www.FionaRoarke.com
facebook.com/FionaRoarke
twitter.com/fiona_roarke

Made in United States
Orlando, FL
29 November 2023

39772014R00154